Copyright © 2011 by Quirk Productions, Inc.
WORST-CASE SCENARIO is a registered trademark of Quirk Productions, Inc.

Visit www.worstcasescenarios.com to learn more about the series.

All rights reserved. No part of this publication may be reproduced in any form without written permission from the publisher.

Library of Congress Cataloging-in-Publication Data available.
ISBN 978-0-8118-7124-2

Book design by Eloise Leigh and Mark Neely.
Typeset in Akzidenz-Grotesk Std.

Manufactured by C & C Offset, Longgang, Shenzhen, China, in May 2011.

10 9 8 7 6 5 4 3 2 1

This product conforms to CPSIA 2008.

Chronicle Books LLC
680 Second Street, San Francisco, California 94107
www.chroniclekids.com

Image credits: Page 189: NASA/JPL/USGS. Page 192: NASA/JPL. Page 194: (top) NASA/MOLA Science Team; (bottom) NASA/JPL. Page 195: (top) NASA/USGS; (center) NASA/JPL/USGS; (bottom) NASA/JPL/USGS. Page 197: NASA/JPL. Page 203: NASA/JPL/Malin Space Science Systems.

WARNING: When a life is at risk or a dangerous situation is at hand, safe alternatives may not exist. The Publisher, Authors, and Consultant disclaim any liability from any injury that may result from the use, proper or improper, of the information contained in this book. All the technical information in this book comes from experts, but we do not guarantee that the information contained herein is complete, safe, or wholly accurate to every scenario, nor should it be considered a substitute for your good judgment or common sense.

The
WORST-CASE SCENARIO

ULTIMATE
ADVENTURE

MARS

YOU DECIDE HOW TO SURVIVE!

By Hena Khan and David Borgenicht
with Robert Zubrin, Mars consultant

Illustrated by Yancey Labat

chronicle books · san francisco

YOU are a member of the Young Astronaut program, handpicked to join a talented international crew on an incredible journey to Mars. Your mission is to:

✦ Arrive on Mars after a six-month ride on the *Fire Star* spacecraft.

✦ Help prepare Mars Base I for its first wave of permanent settlers—and make sure you don't cause any setbacks during your year and a half on the Red Planet.

✦ Get back to Earth after another six-month ride.

At certain points during your adventure, you'll be asked to make choices that will change your story. There are twenty-four possible endings to your mission, but only ONE PATH through the book will fully accomplish your goals.

Before starting your mission, make sure to read the Expedition File at the back of the book, starting on page 189. It's filled with important information you'll need to make wise choices.

You won't be alone on your mission—your fellow astronauts will offer advice and encouragement along the way. But ultimately YOU control your choices and your destiny. So, trust in your good judgment, use the resources you have, and you'll make it to Mars—and back—like a star!

YOUR CREW

JUNIOR ASTRONAUTS

NICOLAS MOREAU
AGE: 14
HOME COUNTRY: FRANCE

Although he goes by Nico for short, this French astronaut isn't short on anything, especially personality. A mechanical whiz, Nico dazzles everyone with his charm and his ability to take machines apart and put them back together. But sometimes Nico can get a little overconfident and carried away with his ideas.

ANEESA MALIK
AGE: 15
HOME COUNTRY: INDIA

Aneesa has never met a circuit she didn't like. The youngest person ever to complete an electrical engineering degree in India, she went on to join the country's space program, where she is a rising star. Aneesa is good at whatever she sets out to do, but she hasn't had to deal with failure much, so her morale could sink if she faces a setback on the ship.

WEN XIANG

AGE: 40   HOME COUNTRY: CHINA

Wen is the commander of the mission. He has a no-nonsense personality, does everything by the book, and demands perfection from his crew. Wen isn't sure how many more missions he will be able to lead before he retires, and he's determined that this one will succeed.

COMMANDER

CREW DOCTOR

COOPER JACKSON

AGE: 33   HOME COUNTRY: U.S.A.

A born daredevil, Cooper joined the space program to fulfill his sense of adventure. Cooper loves surfing, rock climbing, and skydiving, and he's known for taking big risks to get maximum excitement—even if it means getting hurt sometimes. But as the flight surgeon, which is what crew doctors are officially called, he never takes chances with anyone else's health. It's possible, though, that his love of action will make six long months on board a spacecraft very challenging for him.

SCIENTISTS

JULIE DAVIS

AGE: 29   HOME COUNTRY: U.S.A.

A passionate biologist, Julie grew up on a farm in rural Iowa and is happiest around animals. Her shyness disappears if you get her talking about them—then she can go on for hours. Julie is convinced there is life on Mars, and that she will be the one to find it.

VICTORIA ORLOVA

AGE: 38   HOME COUNTRY: RUSSIA

Victoria is a professor of astrophysics at a prestigious university, and really knows her stuff. After years in the space program, she is an expert on many things, and she knows it. Victoria can be your greatest ally, but she doesn't have patience for anything less than your best work.

THE ADVENTURE BEGINS...

MARCH 16, 6:58 A.M.

CAPE CANAVERAL, FLORIDA

"*Fire Star*, you're *go* for launch," says Mission Control.

Your hands sweat as you grip your armrests a little tighter. You're strapped into your seat, leaning completely backward with your legs toward the ceiling. In just one minute, five giant rockets will roar to life underneath you and catapult you into space.

You feel your heart pounding inside your launch suit. You've been training for months for this mission, sitting on simulators, practicing space walks underwater, and studying every system of the spacecraft you're in. You've dreamed of this moment your whole life. And now it's about to happen, sooner than you ever imagined: You are heading to MARS!

"Roger, launch center," says Commander Wen.

"T minus one minute and counting," says Mission Control.

You turn to give thumbs-up to Nico and Aneesa, the other junior astronauts on the crew. The three of you were chosen from thousands of applicants all over the world to be part of this historic mission: to prepare Mars Base I for the first wave of permanent colonists. The goal of the Mars Program is for people of all ages to live on the Red Planet someday, and your mission will prove that young astronauts cannot only make the journey to Mars, but that they can handle important jobs on the base too. There were a lot of skeptics, those who thought that young people had no business in space, let alone on Mars. And you know what? You are *so* ready to prove them wrong!

"*Fire Star*, close and lock your visors, and have a good flight," says Mission Control as the rocket boosters fire up. You close and lock your visor and take a deep breath.

"T MINUS TEN ... NINE ... EIGHT ... "

You imagine the crowds watching outside, waving flags from the five countries involved in the mission, plus all of the people watching on television screens around the world, and you feel a rush of emotion and pride. You *will* be successful on this mission—whatever it takes!

"... SEVEN ... SIX ... FIVE ..."

This is it! You are about to leave planet Earth!

"... FOUR ... THREE ... TWO ... ONE ..."

LIFTOFF!

YOU FEEL A POWERFUL SURGE AS THE SPACECRAFT TEARS OFF THE LAUNCHPAD.

THE FORCE PRESSES YOU BACK INTO YOUR SEAT.

THROUGH A MIRROR, YOU SEE THE GROUND RUSHING AWAY.

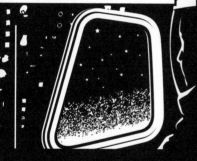

THEN YOU WATCH THE SKY TURN FROM BLUE TO BLACK.

THE RIDE GETS SMOOTHER AS YOU EXIT EARTH'S ATMOSPHERE.

YOU'RE IN SPACE!

WHOO-HOO!!

You're thrilled that you get to share this experience with Nico and Aneesa. After six months of training together, the three of you have become great friends.

Soon, you witness what every astronaut dreams about—the view of Earth from space. It's amazingly beautiful, more than you even imagined, with its bright blue oceans and lush green forests. You can't believe that you won't be back to your home planet for two and a half years. It'll take six months to get to Mars, a year and a half to complete your mission, and another six months to get home. But you're filled with excitement about the adventures waiting for you!

* ✷ .·

Now it's sixty days after launch. You wake up and unstrap yourself from your sleeping bag, which is attached to the wall of the spacecraft. Even after two months in flight to Mars, it still makes you smile to see your fellow astronauts slumbering with their arms floating in front of them, like zombies. But that's what happens in microgravity—if something is not strapped down, it floats.

You've gotten pretty accustomed to using Velcro strips to keep things in place, including yourself. And now you can glide through the cabin like a pro, without bumping into walls or your crewmates.

"Good morning!" says Victoria, the astronaut whose

family picked today's wake-up song, a pop tune from Russia, her home country. The music is broadcast from Mission Control over the intercom, which is known as "com" for short.

Victoria is a smart professor of astrophysics who always keeps you on your toes. She hums along to the music as the two of you head over to the kitchen area, where you find Cooper fixing himself breakfast. Cooper, an American who grew up in California, is a daredevil who is most comfortable on top of a wave, dangling from a cliff, or jumping out of a plane. He loves the physical thrill of being an astronaut, and he's famous for completing the longest space walk in history.

"Eggs over easy, with home fries, please," you joke.

"Nothing I do is easy!" Cooper replies. "Try my protein shake—a few sips of this and you'll be powered up for hours. You might even get through your workout today!"

He shakes his cup and a few drops of chocolate banana smoothie come floating toward you. You expertly catch them in your mouth—*yum*!

As the crew doctor, it's part of Cooper's job to make sure that everyone completes their daily physical fitness routine, which includes activities like "running" while strapped to a treadmill, biking on a stationary machine, and using stretchy bands to keep your muscles in shape. The workouts are required, since your muscles don't do much while you're floating around in microgravity and will become weak if you don't exercise them. Cooper acts like a personal trainer sometimes, pushing you to pedal faster or stretch for longer than you would otherwise.

"Isn't it too early to be talking about workouts?" asks Julie as she floats toward you, rubbing her eyes. Julie is another American crew member, but she's the opposite of Cooper. A biologist and animal lover, her idea of a thrill is watching chicks hatch or milking a cow.

"Never!" responds Cooper with a playful jab. "And if you're lucky, I'll tell you all about the latest findings of my muscle-density project."

Cooper does a lot of side projects in addition to his assigned work on the ship. He likes to keep himself busy, as you've noticed. For his muscle-density project, he's comparing how different types of exercise affect how muscles respond to being in space. You've volunteered your own muscles as "data"—an offer you sometimes regret, because it means that

Cooper *really* cares about your exercise regimen.

You decide to drink one of Cooper's smoothies and see if it really does help you get through your late-morning workout. He's developed a new routine for you and Julie, and he has you both strap your feet to the floor of the compartment to hold yourselves in place. Then, as you bend your legs and turn at the waist, you pull a weighted band back and forth. It seems easy enough at first, until your legs start to burn!

"Faster!" Cooper encourages. "You still have three minutes to go! And then we're gonna hit the bike!"

You spend the next hour biking, sweating, running on the treadmill, and sweating some more. Finally, the workout is over. Cooper gives you a thump on the back.

"Good job, superstar! You hung in there, and you earned your shower."

You've never been more grateful that the *Fire Star* is equipped with a real shower, although everyone is limited to showering for two minutes every two days because of the limited water supply. You can't imagine what life used to be like on board the International Space Station years ago, when astronauts had no showers at all and had to stay clean using only dry shampoo and baby wipes.

After a quick but refreshing shower, you spend the rest of the afternoon upgrading a computer system, which is your assignment for the day. Cooper is in the command module with you, and he's designing new workouts, checking medical records, and working on his muscle-density project. You wonder when he's going to get to his assignment for the day—he's supposed to monitor the ship's ventilation system, which includes replacing filters that remove dirt, dust, and bacteria from your breathing air, and any defective fans, which keep the air circulating.

"Five minutes to our evening briefing," says Commander Wen over com.

During the evening briefings, everyone runs through their tasks and gives updates on their progress. Every person on the crew has to help with checking, cleaning, and maintaining all of the systems on board. It's not the most glamorous work, and it gets boring sometimes to repeat the same things over and over, but it's essential. Any small malfunction could mean serious problems for the spacecraft and the crew.

You hurry to the meeting. Commander Wen runs a tight ship, and you never want to be late. You're not as intimidated by the highest-ranking astronaut, from China, as you were when you first met him. Now that you've gotten to know him, you think he's really kind and fair. But you still work hard to impress him.

"What's the bacon shakin'?" asks Nico as you take your place next to him. Nico is French, and you laugh at his mix-up of the American expression you taught him.

"You mean, 'what's shakin', bacon?'" you say, but then he winks and you realize that he's just kidding.

That's Nico—always making everyone laugh, even if it means making fun of himself, and definitely if it means making fun of others! But he's so good-natured about it, no one ever minds. He is also a mechanical mastermind, and can be found tinkering with a robot or a spare part during any free time.

You and Aneesa exchange smiles. Aneesa is a bit more serious, but supersmart, and one of the best problem solvers you've ever met.

"Let's get started," Commander Wen says, looking down at the list of jobs on his clipboard. "How's the ventilation system, Cooper?" he asks.

Cooper looks up, startled to be called on first.

"Um, yeah . . . it's fine," he mumbles. You steal a glance at Cooper, who doesn't look at you. The two of you spent most of the day together, and you never saw him monitoring anything. You wonder when he could have done his job, and if he made all the filter and fan replacements that were needed.

"How's the computer system update going?" Commander Wen asks you next, interrupting your thoughts.

"Complete," you report back.

Commander Wen nods in approval and continues making his way down the list of jobs. The meeting wraps up with everyone rushing off to finish their work before dinner.

"Hey, Cooper, do you need a hand with the ventilation system?" you offer as you head out.

"Uh, that's okay, superstar. It's no big deal," Cooper responds.

But you don't see him anywhere near the monitoring station the rest of the day.

Later that night, you can't get this nagging thought out of your head: When Cooper said the monitoring was "no big deal," did he mean that he didn't think it was *important*? Could he have skipped it? You admit to yourself, it *is* tempting to skip your routine jobs sometimes, especially when the work gets tedious, but it still has to get done.

You look over at Cooper, who is busily recording updates about the crew's health. You know he works hard, but it seems like he always focuses on the work that he *likes*—the workouts, his side projects, medical stuff. If he is skipping the ventilation monitoring, it's serious—he could be putting the whole crew at risk. On a spacecraft, you can't just open up a window to get some fresh air—you need the ventilation system to be in perfect working order so you all can breathe.

You're not sure what to do. You could just ask Cooper again if he did the monitoring. But as a junior crew member, you don't know how he'll react. He's been on several missions before, so he has experience on his side. Plus, he outranks you, so he might not appreciate being nagged.

Going straight to Commander Wen is out of the question. He's so busy, he'd never want you to bother him with something you hadn't tried to handle on your own first. Part of you thinks it might be easier to just check Cooper's work log and see if he recorded anything. If he hasn't, you can keep offering to "help" him until he gets it done. If he really won't do anything, *then* you can go to Commander Wen. The risk is that if Cooper finds out you peeked in his log, he might get angry at you for snooping. But that's only if he catches you. The log is easy to access right over there at the command module, and Cooper seems like he'll be working elsewhere for a while. What do you choose?

IF YOU CONFRONT COOPER DIRECTLY ABOUT HIS WORK, TURN TO PAGE 89.

IF YOU TAKE A PEEK AT HIS LOG WHEN HE ISN'T LOOKING, TURN TO PAGE 112.

"Okay, let's do it!" you tell Nico. You follow the blueprint designs that he comes up with and, with his help, make the changes to the telerobots. This includes adding new front wheels, which allow for 360-degree rotation, using bigger tires, adjusting the gearing, and installing an extra battery pack for more power. Meanwhile, Nico works on the body of the robots, making them a lot lighter and sleeker and more like race cars.

"They look so cool!" you say when you're done.

"Well, let's see what they can do," Nico says.

You create a course for the robots to race, and line them up at the start line.

"Winner gets to take the rest of the day off, and the loser has to do both of our assignments," Nico adds.

You put your finger on the accelerator button, waiting for the clock to tick down. Three . . . two . . . one . . . go!

Nico's robot takes a quick lead, but yours starts to catch up after a few seconds. They are soon neck and neck and about to turn the next corner when, suddenly, you lose control of your robot. It swipes Nico's robot, causing them both to go off course and straight into a wall at high speed.

A few second later, you
and Nico are staring at a tangled
mess of metal parts. The robots are
in pieces, and so are your reputations as
hardworking, serious junior astronauts. Your
reckless driving just cost the Mars Program
thousands of dollars in damages. The only thing
racing now is your heart, as you imagine telling
Commander Wen about the accident, and thinking about
what the consequences will be. Talk about crash and burn!

THE END

Three weeks later, you've learned more about goats than you ever wanted to know. You've memorized the name and age of each of the seventeen goats in the dome-shaped greenhouse they inhabit. You've observed their eating habits—which basically amounts to devouring anything and everything they can get to—and figured out that they always smell really, really bad.

You wonder about the reasoning of the scientists whose idea it was to bring goats to breed on Mars for their milk, fur, and meat. They eat so much and cause so much damage by

chewing through stuff that it might not be worth it to keep them around in the long run. But that's where your job comes in—you're supposed to track the goats' weight, food intake, and all their habits so a future decision can be made about the breeding program. You've been keeping a detailed log of each goat's actions, including their naps and bathroom habits. *Yawn!*

Frankly, you're starting to get a little bit jealous of Nico, who's been telling you each night at dinner about his exciting expeditions. The latest is that he was lucky enough to get a ride on a scouting plane over the Martian terrain.

"We got to see the Valles Marineris, and it was awesome!" he told you last night. Valles Marineris is the biggest known canyon in the entire solar system, which makes the Grand Canyon on Earth look like nothing more than a little crack! You can't wait to see it.

All you could report back was how many times Sophie (yes, that's one of the goat's names) had butted her sister Coco in the head.

Now it's late morning, and you're leaning against the wall of the goat facility imagining that you're on a scouting mission. You're soaring over the Martian frontier in a plane, getting an aerial view of the famous Valles Marineris canyon, and then . . .

BAAA!

You're rudely awakened by Bubba, your least favorite goat. Bubba always seems to be the hungry one, who feels the need to remind you that it's time to eat. You much prefer goats like Coco who never get bossy or pushy at feeding time.

Come to think of it, where is Coco anyway? You haven't seen her in a while, and quickly go through goat roll call. Sophie, Brent, Heidi, Zara, Ashley, Jacob, Miles, Hans, Yao, Vladimir, Anna, Farid, Edward, Luca, Rosco, Bubba . . . but . . . no Coco!

You run through the list a second time and check all the name tags, but Coco is still missing. Where could she have gone? Then you see a small hole at the back of the pen. She must have chewed through the wall and snuck out!

You can't believe you have managed to lose a goat. You race around the greenhouse, but don't see the goat anywhere. As you're running, you bump into Julie, who's studying some ferns.

"Hey, partner! What's the hurry?" she asks.

Julie might be able to help you find the missing goat. She's really great with animals, since she grew up on a farm. But, if you admit that you messed up on the easiest job around, how will you ever be trusted to go on an expedition, which is much more challenging? Maybe it's better to just try to find the goat on your own.

IF YOU TELL JULIE ABOUT THE MISSING GOAT, TURN TO PAGE 101.

IF YOU KEEP SEARCHING ON YOUR OWN, TURN TO PAGE 36.

You're having an amazing time playing in the Mars Flight Basketball League. You hardly think about the expedition that you missed, and you don't mind too much when the days go by and you still aren't invited on another one. While watching the basketball team do all sorts of crazy acrobatics while shooting the ball, you get the idea of starting up an official gymnastics troupe. Maybe with Nico's help, you can build an enormous trampoline!

The next morning you go to check on Nico, who is still busy working on the telerobots in the warehouse. You're hoping you can get him excited about the idea of the gymnastics troupe.

"Hey, Nico!" you say. "I was wondering if you have time to help me build a giant trampoline for the recreation dome."

"A what?" he asks you.

"A trampoline. You know . . . the big things that people jump on? Like for gymnastics?" you reply.

"I know what a trampoline is! I'm just surprised that you're asking me right now. Do you know how much work we still have to get done? Man!" he mutters.

Wow. You're surprised by the tone of his voice. Nico is usually so friendly. Maybe he's a little bitter that he's been stuck working with the telerobots and hasn't been able to have as much fun as you've had recently. You make a note to invite him to try out the new trampoline after you find a way to build it.

But you never get a chance. A few days later, Commander Wen comes to see you, looking grave.

"I've noticed a pattern that concerns me. First you chose basketball game over going on a resource expedition. Now you're focusing your efforts on recreation, not work. Is that right?" he asks.

"Um, I did take some time off, but—" is all you can stammer.

"Every person on this team is essential to the success of this mission," Commander Wen interrupts. "Everyone must work extremely hard. You may have already put our mission behind schedule. I'm afraid this is going on your record and could affect the decision to keep you in the program going forward."

You're back on goat duty until Commander Wen decides you're ready to prove yourself. You can forget basketball. For the next two months you'll only be dribbling, shooting, and slam-dunking with a team of eighteen smelly four-footed animals. Game over.

THE END

"What's up?" Julie asks you when you don't initially respond.

"Um, nothing! That compost looks great. See you later!" you say, and then dash off, leaving Julie wondering what's going on.

You search the greenhouse high and low, and can't find the missing goat anywhere. Finally, when you're about to give up, you spot a furry little tail sticking out from behind a crate.

"Aha! I've got you!" you say, taking a step closer.

Coco turns around and sees you approaching. You look straight into her big brown eyes and beckon her in a hushed voice. Then you see another little head peek out—it's a new baby goat! Coco obviously snuck off to give birth. *Wow!*

"Coco! Coco! Come here, girl!"

She looks at you a moment longer, starts to take a step toward you, and then . . . bolts in the opposite direction. The baby goat takes off after her. You've been watching the goats for a while now, but you've *never* seen any move that fast or bounce so high! In the lower Martian gravity, Coco and her kid seem to be flying with each step, and as you chase behind them, you hope no one can see you scrambling after hopping goats!

You are panting, out of breath, and ready to quit when you see what you feared most—Coco is heading toward Julie's prized prehistoric species seedlings. *No!* She could eat her way through those in no time! You have to move fast and get her. What should you do—try to scare her into running away from the garden, or let her nibble on a precious plant and sneak up behind her and grab her collar?

IF YOU DECIDE TO SCARE HER, TURN TO PAGE 176.

IF YOU DECIDE TO SNEAK UP BEHIND HER, TURN TO PAGE 76.

As night begins to fall and there is *still* no sign of the rescue team, you, Cooper, and Victoria huddle around the rover. You use the cables from the vehicle to plug your space suits into the power source, which, luckily, still has enough fuel in it to keep running. Then you crank up your suits to the maximum heat setting to get you through the incredibly cold night. To avoid draining the power of the rover, you turn off the lights and sit in the blackness of the Martian night. And wow, is it dark! Even though Mars has two moons, they don't offer much in the way of light like Earth's moon. Cooper and Victoria are just a couple feet away from you, but you can hardly make out their shapes.

"We sure could use a campfire," you say.

"Do you guys wanna tell ghost stories?" Cooper jokes.

"This is scary enough already," Victoria replies. "Let's get some rest and hope for a rescue team in the morning."

Early the next morning, you wake up grateful that the rover kept your suits powered up through the night. You hear a sound, and you look up to see another rover approaching. It's a rescue team!

As the rover gets closer, you can see Nico and several others waving at you. You've been found!

"Thank goodness!" Victoria shouts, pulling the plug out of her space suit.

"Are you guys okay?" Nico asks as he jumps out of the rover. "We were so worried!"

"We're okay," you answer. "But Cooper and Victoria are injured. We need to get them back to base as quickly as possible."

"Let's get moving, then," Nico says. "Don't worry. You guys will be safe at home soon!"

You know what he means, but you still can't help thinking, *it's not really home.*

* ✳ ·

Back at base an hour later, you are greeted like heroes by the rest of the crew. You realize that even though your expedition went bust, the fact that you survived is reason enough to celebrate. But once all of the excitement and relief at being back safely is over, you can't stop replaying the accident and the experience of being stranded over and over in your mind. You are really shaken up by it, and it's made you extremely homesick . . . for your real home, on Earth. You decide you don't want to go on another expedition again. You really just want to get back to the planet you know and love best. In the meantime, you'll do what you can to help out the Mars Program, but you let Commander Wen know that you'd like to hitch a ride on the next supply ship headed home.

THE END

You set off in the direction of the distant lights of the Mars settlement. The faint light of your wristwatch glows slightly, giving the Martian landscape an eerie, haunted feeling. If you believed in alien monsters, you'd be pretty scared right now! *But luckily I don't believe in alien monsters,* you say to yourself. You step carefully over the rocks you can see, stumble occasionally over a few that you don't, but manage to stay on your feet and to make slow progress.

You can't wait to get back to the settlement and finally send help for your friends. But at this point, you are thinking of yourself, too—dreaming of changing out of this bulky space suit into some comfy sweats, drinking some hot chocolate, and getting a good night's sleep. You don't remember ever being this physically or mentally exhausted in your life.

After you've been walking for about fifteen minutes, the lights you are heading toward don't seem to be getting any closer. But the light on your watch is growing dimmer. This battery is starting to die too! You quickly try to pick up the pace, before it runs out completely.

Suddenly your boot hits a small ditch you didn't see. You trip and start to fall, and put your arms out to catch yourself from landing flat on your face. You manage to prevent a major impact, but hear a very scary sound. *CRACK!*

Not alien monsters, but worse. It's the sound of your helmet hitting a rock and your visor cracking ever so slightly. Unfortunately, a crack is all it takes. As the pressure in your suit drops, your body cramps from the effects of rapid decompression, and you lose consciousness. You're lucky you won't feel what happens next.

THE END

You feel a little bad for rejecting Nico's plan, but you don't want to take any chances with dynamite.

"We'll come back with a larger team and see what they think about extracting the ice," you promise.

"Don't worry about it," Nico says good-naturedly. The rest of the way back to base, you eagerly chat about how excited the team is going to be about the big discovery. And they *are* excited! Commander Wen immediately organizes a follow-up team to go out and mine both the ice and the permafrost you've uncovered.

"This is really going to help expand our water supply," he tells you with a look of pride. "Good work!"

But then he goes on to tell you that you're going to be building bricks for your next assignment, and not going out with the follow-up team.

"But sir, shoudn't I help finish the job?" you ask.

"You've done your part, and we'll take it from here. Remember, we all have to rotate between the expeditions and routine work," he replies.

You're pretty disappointed, but guess he does have a point. You can't expect to cruise the Martian landscape and make discoveries *every* day, can you?

TURN TO PAGE 187.

You set up a remote camera and do a survey of the damaged habitation compartment from your computer. It's clear that the fire burned out a control panel, which is probably what shorted out the communications system. Moving the camera closer to the sides of the spacecraft, you examine the blackened walls. It seems that Aneesa's initial feeling was correct—that everything's okay and that the black film is just from the smoke and will easily wipe clean.

"Everything is checking out fine on my end," Aneesa says. "I think we're ready to repressurize."

"Hold on. I just need to inspect one more thing," you say. You measure the curve of the spacecraft walls to check for thinning, and the reading comes out in the normal range.

"It's normal. What do you think?"

"We've got to get the crew out!" she says. "Let's do this!"

You can't help but feel that Aneesa is rushing things, and part of you wishes you had just gone on the space walk, but it's too late now. Your mind races through all of the checks that you did as Aneesa starts the repressurizing. And then you suddenly realize what you forgot to do—check the exterior of the spacecraft using laser sensor imaging.

"Aneesa . . . wait!" you shout. But you're too late. The laser sensor imager would have alerted you to the fact that the heat from the fire warped a couple areas, which knocked some tiles off the spacecraft. You also would have spotted the damage if you'd gone on your space walk. But now you realize too late that the weakened walls of the spacecraft can't contain the pressure of the gas. Suddenly there's a gaping hole in the side of the ship, and the next thing you know, there's a giant explosion. *Fire Star* is breaking up . . .

THE END

YOU FIND NORTH USING CYGNUS
AND CEPHEUS AS YOUR GUIDES.

YOU KEEP MOVING, BUT EVERY
STEP GETS HEAVIER.

YOU EASE YOURSELF DOWN INTO A SMALL CRATER.

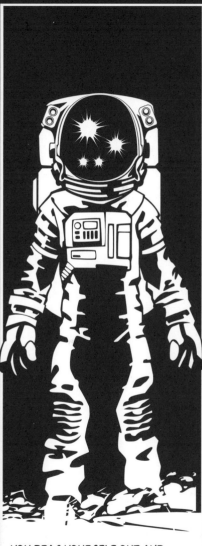

YOU DRAG YOURSELF OUT, AND THEN YOU SEE...

Lights! That means that the Mars Colony is only about a mile up ahead! You almost want to shout with happiness, and start to jog back to the base.

But as you hurry along, your flashlight starts to flicker. *Uh-oh.* Then, it goes out. *Argh!* What horrible timing! You've come so far and are in the homestretch, only to be slowed down again by, of all things, a stinking battery.

You need some light to make your way back, or else you'll be fumbling over rocks and craters in the dark. Luckily, you were trained on how to tap into your space suit's power reserves for emergency use. If you sit down and try to work it, you could wire the flashlight to your suit and get enough juice to light your way back to base. But it'll take time to get

everything connected, especially because it's been a while since you went through the exercise, and you'll have to work by the faint light of your wristwatch.

Wait a minute. You look down at your watch. What if you forget the flashlight and just use the light of the watch to guide you? It's not very bright, but it could be enough to help you for just the short distance you have left. And you really don't want to delay getting back any longer.

IF YOU TAP INTO YOUR SPACE SUIT FOR POWER, TURN TO PAGE 107.

IF YOU TRAVEL BY THE LIGHT OF YOUR WATCH, TURN TO PAGE 41.

You take photographs and video of the rock with the telerobot, make careful notes of your location, and collect samples of soil and other rocks in the area. But your mind isn't really on your work—you can't wait to tell Julie about your discovery and bring a team to visit this site.

Back at base, you find Julie in the laboratory and show her everything.

"Wow," she says, but then adds, "It's really hard for me to confirm much with just this. I'll talk to Commander Wen and see if we can put another expedition together. Are you confident that it'll be worth it?"

"Yes," you reply. Although with every passing moment, you feel a little less sure.

Commander Wen approves the expedition. On the drive out to the spot, you imagine the look of amazement on Julie's face when she sees the rock, and the pride in Commander Wen's voice when he commends you for spotting a universe-shattering discovery!

The rover pulls up to the location you've marked and everyone piles out, carrying loads of equipment like cameras, rock cutters, extractors, and containers. You lead the team over to the rock and point to the stromatolite with a flourish.

"That's it?" Julie asks, peering down at the rock.

"Yes," you reply.

"Hmm," Julie says. You hold your breath for what's coming next.

And then Julie starts to laugh—really hard. "This isn't a stromatolite," she gasps between giggles, before she manages to calm down. "Ivan and Helena could've told you that right away."

Yikes. You look over at Commander Wen, and he hasn't cracked a smile.

"This is no laughing matter. Do you know how many resources were wasted on this wild-goose chase? Fuel, manpower, lost time . . ."

You should have known better. In your quest for a discovery, you were too eager. Now, you'll be making up for the losses to the mission by working overtime, making bricks for habitats for a long time.

TURN TO PAGE 187.

Almost two hours later, you are standing in your space suit. It's so stiff that it's difficult to move around. Your suit has a life-support system, which lets you breathe, keeps you cool, gives you power, and allows you to communicate with the spacecraft. You're wearing a nitrogen-propelled backpack

that'll let you fly around the spacecraft if necessary, using hand controllers to steer. To keep you from drifting away into space, you're attached to a cable that is tethered to the spacecraft.

Tethered to you, in turn, are five space suits, one for each of your stranded crewmates. The suits don't weigh anything, of course, so it'll be no problem to drag them along behind you. You just hope that you won't get tangled up with them, and you make sure that the tether is secure. Now you are as ready as you're ever going to be for this space walk!

"How do I look?" you ask Aneesa, who helped you get into your suit.

"Like the fifteen million bucks your space suit cost!" Aneesa says, giving your gloved hand a fist bump. "Go get 'em, partner!"

You step into the air lock, which is an airtight chamber between the spacecraft and the outside. With the turn of a switch, you depressurize the air lock. A few minutes later, you close your eyes and open the hatch.

You open your eyes, and there it is in front of you: the awesome blackness of space. *Unbelievable!* This isn't how you imagined your first space walk would happen, but even with all the stress of your emergency mission, it's still incredibly thrilling to step out alone into the universe.

"Nice work!" says Commander Wen, patting you on the shoulder.

"You did it!" cheers Julie, with tears in her eyes.

"That was awesome!" says Nico.

"I'm really impressed, superstar!" adds Cooper, with a thump you can feel through your pressurized suit.

"Are you feeling okay?" asks Victoria.

Actually, you feel great. Better than great. You're so grateful that everything went smoothly and that you were able to get to your crewmates safely. Now you can all work together to get the spacecraft back in order. You proudly accept when Commander Wen asks you to lead the group on the space walk back to the other side of the ship. And this time, you get to take your time and enjoy the view.

It turns out that the damage to the spacecraft is minimal, and since you wisely waited to repressurize the habitation module until Commander Wen had done all the necessary stress tests and repairs, the compartment holds up just fine when you refill it with air. Everyone is hugely relieved to have a fully up-and-running spacecraft again!

The next few months of space travel are uneventful, but in a good way. There are no more catastrophes and no need for daring rescues, just your daily work and the regular routines of astronaut life. But after six months of being confined to the spacecraft, you are more than ready to explore the great frontier of Mars— and to experience all the adventures the next year and a half will bring.

And now, your much awaited landing on the Red Planet is about to happen!

The crew is huddled around the windows of the spacecraft, watching the reddish-orange-hued sphere that is Mars come into view. You can see the craters and canyons that you've only seen in photos before, and you're completely awestruck. You can't wait to get out there and start exploring!

"We have entered the atmosphere of Mars," Commander Wen announces amid the celebration of the crew. "Strap yourselves in, everyone. We are *go* to land."

You attach your safety belts and wait with a pounding heart for the landing sequence.

YOU FEEL TRIPLE GRAVITY AS THE SPACECRAFT PLOWS INTO THE MARTIAN ATMOSPHERE.

YOU HEAR *FIRE STAR* THROW OFF ITS HEAT SHIELD.

YOU FEEL A JOLT AS THE DESCENT PARACHUTE DEPLOYS.

THE THRUST OF THE ROCKETS TELLS YOU THE SPACECRAFT IS READY TO TOUCH DOWN.

When the spacecraft doors are opened, you step out into
a large elevator compartment that will lower you to ground
level, where a transport rover awaits you. Fortunately, the
elevator has enormous windows, because this is where you
get your first glimpse of Mars! You gasp as you look outside.
You see the impressive domes of Mars Base I, your home

for the next year and a half. Beyond the base, you see a vast red desert stretching all the way to the horizon. You stare at the pale pinkish-yellowish Martian sky, so different from Earth's blue sky. *Wow.* You could look at this scene for hours, but soon, you've reached ground level, and it's time to climb aboard the transport rover for the short ride to the spaceport.

Your remote-controlled transport rover glides across the soil and through the airlock doors, which slide shut behind you. You're inside the base! You and the rest of the crew climb off the rover and smile as you greet the first new people you've seen in six months.

"Greetings, Earthlings," jokes Oscar Schweiger, the Chief Mars Settlement Officer. "Welcome to Mars. We hope you enjoy your time here as Martians."

Martians. Even though that's what Mars residents are called, for some reason the word still makes you think of green cartoon characters with antennae and laser guns.

Over the next few hours, you meet the staff that has been setting up the Mars Colony for the past year. They have done a lot of important groundwork, like constructing basic housing, building the first greenhouse, and going on the first expeditions to explore for materials needed to make longer term settlements on Mars possible.

Your crew's job is to help take the new colony to the next level, expanding the base by building bigger and stronger habitats and other important buildings, making sure the food supply is stable, and searching for resources you'll need for energy and construction. If you succeed, the first wave of colonists will soon arrive to start permanent residence on Mars—the ultimate goal of the Mars Program.

"Can you believe we're really here?" Nico asks you during a break from the introductions. "I can't wait to get out and explore this place!"

"Me too. I hope we're on the same expedition team!" you reply, eager to get into a rover and out into the frontier.

Commander Wen calls out your first assignments.

"Nico and Cooper, expedition for fuel sources. Victoria, construction of recreation dome. Aneesa, central dome for communication system updates." And then you hear your name.

"Greenhouse dome for goat duty." *What?* Did you hear that right?

"Excuse me, sir. Can you repeat that?" you ask.

"You'll be tending to the goats in the greenhouse," Wen repeats. *Seriously?* Babysitting goats? You thought you'd be doing something a *lot* more exciting than that.

Cooper sees the expression on your face and pulls you aside after the meeting.

"Hey, superstar, I know you were hoping for a field expedition assignment, but this is a good way for you to show everyone how you always have a good attitude and work hard, even when you don't like your task."

"Yeah, I guess so. Thanks for the pep talk," you reply, trying to hide your disappointment.

You start to head over to the greenhouse to meet your furry new friends when you overhear Victoria and Aneesa speaking.

"Nico is so lucky that he was chosen to go on an expedition already!" Aneesa is saying.

"Well, he must have really impressed Commander Wen to be picked for such a challenging job," Victoria replies.

Wait a minute. Nico's great and all, but why is *he* the one who impressed Commander Wen? You were the one who rescued the crew with a space walk on the trip over here. Wasn't that impressive enough? You feel your face get hot as you think about how unfair this is! You've been dying to get out into the Martian frontier and explore after being cooped up on a spacecraft for six months. You wonder if you should politely ask Commander Wen for a new assignment. Maybe he'll realize his mistake and even appreciate your pointing it out. Or should you take Cooper's suggestion to just go along with what you've got and hope for something better next time?

IF YOU ASK COMMANDER WEN TO REASSIGN YOU, TURN TO PAGE 84.

IF YOU KEEP WALKING TO THE GREENHOUSE, TURN TO PAGE 30.

You show Aneesa how to strap on her wings, and then put on your own.

"You flap them like this, and then let them catch on the air. . . " you begin. But you hardly need to say anything else, because Aneesa was apparently born to fly and takes off before you finish your sentence.

"This is *am-a-zing*!" she sings as she soars by you.

You can't agree more, although you *do* have a little pang of guilt about Nico not being able to join in on the fun. But that feeling is quickly replaced by excitement when you and Aneesa take a rest and talk about the next big plans for the recreation dome.

"Did you hear that they're going to put up basketball nets?" Aneesa asks.

That's a slam-dunk idea if you've ever heard one! Playing basketball in the pressurized dome would take the game to new heights, literally.

"You could jump over the head of any basketball player in this gravity!" you marvel.

"I know, and if you put on wings, you could actually *fly* to the hoop!" Aneesa adds.

"Yeah, but wouldn't that be cheating?" you argue.

As you continue debating the rules of the game, Cooper comes by.

"I'm glad to hear you guys so enthusiastic about the sports leagues we're setting up. Would you be willing to be in charge of the basketball committee?" he asks you both.

"Sure!" you reply.

"I'd be glad to help out," Aneesa says, "if I have enough time left after my work."

You're more than ready to trade in a little more work to help set up the league. Over the next week, you throw yourself into organizing the teams, setting the game schedules, firming up the rules, and even choosing the colors of the teams' uniforms. This is going to be awesome!

Tonight is the first Mars Flight Basketball League game, and your team—the Marvelous Martians—is scheduled to play. You've been practicing and have mastered a beautiful layup with a somersault in the middle—and you can't wait to show it off. Your team is looking good, and you're sure you're going to win.

But two hours before tip-off, you get a call from Commander Wen. "I've got an expedition team assembled and ready to go scouting for mineral resources, and we could use an extra set of hands. I meant to ask you earlier, and I'm not sure if you have the time, but if so, we'd love to have you join us."

Finally! This is your first expedition opportunity, and you've been waiting for it for a long time. You've been waiting to get out into the Martian frontier and have some adventures that don't involve goats. But what terrible timing! You really want to play in the first game of the basketball league that you've worked so hard to set up. It's going to be so much fun, and if your team wins, you get to play again tomorrow.

IF YOU ACCEPT THE EXPEDITION OFFER, TURN TO PAGE 68.

IF YOU PASS ON THIS TRIP AND PLAY IN THE GAME, TURN TO PAGE 34.

You hurry to join the expedition team, which is already assembled. You're a little disappointed that none of your crewmates will be accompanying you. Instead, you're with a couple of Martian scientists you don't know very well named Ivan and Helena. The three of you will be exploring for mineral resources in a pressurized rover, using telerobots to collect specimens for you.

Even though you'd rather share the moment with your friends, it's thrilling to be getting off the base, and as you drive away from the settlement, you're amazed all over again by the fact that you are on Mars.

"It's pretty impressive, eh?" asks Ivan. "I still can't believe I'm here, after six months already."

You wonder if you'll ever get used to the feeling of looking out onto the rocky reddish-colored landscape. It's awesome.

Collecting the samples is fun, and you enjoy using the remote controller to steer the telerobots and watching their

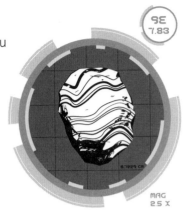

movements through a camera. You command a robot to scoop up samples and dump them into a canister in the rover. Then, while you are steering the robot past a big rock, something catches your eye. Unlike all the other dust-covered rocks you've been seeing, this one stands out because of a distinct pattern on it. You move the telerobot back and forth over the rock, peering closely at the image that is transmitted. Why does that look so familiar? You've seen this pattern before, if you could just remember where. *Wait a minute!* This rock looks similar to images you've studied of stromatolites, the earliest fossils ever discovered on Earth.

Could it be? Could you really have just found a stromatolite? *No way!* Scientists have been combing over Mars with telerobots for decades, and have recently been going on manned expeditions, to search for any evidence of fossil life on the planet. The debate about whether or not there is, or was, life on Mars has been raging for decades. Although several scientists have come close to big breakthroughs, there has *never* been any proof.

With your heart pounding, you review what you know

about stromatolites. These rich fossils have tons of tiny organisms stuck in them, and they take thousands of years to form. They've been used to understand the role that ancient organisms, stuff like blue-green algae, play in the evolution of life on Earth. Most stromatolites you've seen have strips of light and dark colors running across them. You look at the rock again closely, and see the same color pattern. *Whoa.* If this is really a stromatolite, it will rock the scientific world!

You can't believe that you might have just stumbled upon a major discovery like this. You look over at Ivan and Helena, and for some reason, you don't feel comfortable sharing your find with them. Even though they're perfectly nice, you hardly know them, and you aren't sure how they will react to you. What if you're wrong? You'd rather show Julie and the other members of your team first to get their input. Not to mention, you'd rather share the excitement of the potential discovery with *them*, not with Ivan and Helena. You wonder if you should get the robot to take a sample of the rock, and then show it to Julie. Or you could just take careful note of where you are and bring Julie back to check it out.

IF YOU TAKE A SAMPLE NOW, TURN TO PAGE 85.

IF YOU PLAN TO BRING JULIE BACK WITH YOU ANOTHER TIME, TURN TO PAGE 50.

You take cover behind the boulder and wait. In a matter of minutes, you see an enormous reddish-pink cloud heading your way. *Whoa!* This is the start of a full-fledged dust storm! You're so glad you didn't try to walk through that mess—you wouldn't have been able to see anything or get anywhere!

Crouched next to the boulder with grains of sand scouring your suit, you wonder how long this storm is going to last. Unfortunately, you know that Martian dust storms can last for months. *Months!* Thinking about that makes your stomach queasy. A lot is unknown about Martian dust storms—no one knows how to predict them, so you couldn't have known about this before you started your trek. It was just plain old bad luck.

But fortunately, your luck turns around.

After what seems like forever, but is actually only about two hours, the storm dies down. Before you know it, the air is calm, and the dust is settling—and a lot of it has settled on you! If anyone saw you walking around, they'd think a pile of sand came to life. You use a cloth to wipe off your visor, and you shake off as much dust as you can. Then you look around.

The sun is setting, and in the dim light of dusk, you can see that the rover tracks you were following are no longer there! Like a giant sandbox that has been shaken, the desert floor has lost all marks and grooves. You realize you don't know which way to go.

As you try to orient yourself, the sky grows darker, and you become more nervous. Will you have to spend the night alone on the Martian frontier? But then, the stars begin to appear. *The stars!* You can use what you know about constellations to guide yourself back to base!

On Mars, you can find the same constellations you can see from Earth. The only thing that's a little different is how you find the Martian "north star," which is a point halfway between Deneb and Alderamin. Fortunately, the materials you got during your training gave you a little crash course on navigating at night on Mars. Now you just have to remember . . .

THE VIEW TO
YOUR LEFT

IF YOU GO TO THE LEFT, TURN TO PAGE 46.

... AND THE VIEW
TO YOUR RIGHT

IF YOU GO TO THE RIGHT, TURN TO PAGE 147.

You wait until Coco has taken a nice mouthful of prehistoric plant and is contentedly chewing on it. Slowly, you creep up behind her and thrust your hand onto her collar—got her! Coco starts bleating and kicking, but you hold on tightly and drag her out of the garden.

"Oh no! What's this?" you hear Julie cry out. You look up and find her looking at the chewed plant, shaking her head.

"I'm so sorry, Julie," you pant, out of breath from fighting with the goat. "This goat got out of the pen, but I chased her down before she could do more damage."

"You should have let me help you when I offered—I have dog biscuits that we could have used to get her to come to us. That would have been smarter than chasing her, silly!"

Julie is an animal expert—you should have trusted her to help you.

"I know, I messed up," you say. "But look, there's a new kid. Coco just gave birth!"

"Aw, it's beautiful," Julie says. "I can't believe we didn't notice that Coco was pregnant!"

After the two of you spend a few minutes petting the baby goat, Julie says, "Listen, why don't you let me take over watching the goats for you. I know they need some help over in building materials. It's not the most exciting work, but it's important."

You get the feeling that Julie is trying to get rid of you, but you think you're going to take her up on the offer just the same. You've had more excitement than you bargained for in the greenhouse. Building materials sounds pretty good right about now, even if it's not an expedition.

TURN TO PAGE 187.

You head to the science station and make sure no one is around. So far, so good. Then you check the rovers parked outside to see if they have the same fuel tanks as your model. *Bingo!* This is going to work! You start to remove the fuel tank from one of the rovers. Once it's off, you'll just switch it with the empty one from your rover. Simple enough.

Except . . . as you start to lift out the fuel tank from the other rover, you hear an alarm go off. You try to take the tank out anyway, but it won't release.

"Let's try to disconnect the alarm," Julie suggests.

You look at the wires of the alarm and aren't sure what to do. But how hard can it be to disable the alarm? As you're fiddling with the wires, you cross two of them that shouldn't be mixed. *ZAP!* The last thing you remember is feeling a massive jolt of electricity running through your body, and falling backward. When you finally wake up, you're told you are lucky to be alive. But you have some lingering side effects of near electrocution—your heart beat is irregular, and you have nerve damage. You're going to be sent home as soon as possible to be properly treated by a neurologist. Unfortunately, the shock of going back to Earth without finishing the mission is going to take even longer to wear off!

THE END

You watch as everyone scrambles to prepare for the emergency shutdown. You all gather around the lead scientist, who pulls a lever, sending rods into the core of the generator and stopping the nuclear reactions. Within four seconds, the generator is shut down. *Whump.* You hear silence as systems around the base turn off, powerless.

"Disaster averted," Commander Wen announces. "We got the generator turned off just in time."

"Yes, but now let's see if we can get it going again," Aneesa mutters under her breath. You look at her, surprised.

"I think the shutdown was a bad idea," she whispers. "Once it cools down and depressurizes, we'll have to start testing, and it'll take several days to get things going again."

You tell her about your idea to use the robot to clean the dust, and wonder if you should have suggested it after all.

"I can't believe you didn't at least mention it!" she says.

Now you *really* wish you did.

Over the next few days, the base operates on reserve power, and everyone conserves energy as much as they can. And then you hear the news that Aneesa feared: the shutdown caused a malfunction in the generator, and it won't be starting up again anytime soon! The generator needs a new part to arrive on the next shipment from Earth. Now the base has to come up with an alternative energy option in the next week, before your reserve power supply runs out. Even though geothermal power sources would be the best short-term solution, since it taps into the natural heat sources deep below the surface of Mars, searching for it and extracting it could take months. *We've got just one week.*

Everyone is debating the fastest energy options: to put up more solar panels or to build windmills. Commander Wen calls a special meeting to decide, and the room erupts into loud disagreements over which path to take. Those in favor

of solar panels argue that they can be put up quickly and are a proven energy source, even if they have low output at times. The windmill supporters think that solar panels haven't provided enough power on their own to fuel the base, and that if you rely on both the sun *and* wind, you'll have power no matter what the weather is like. Finally, Commander Wen quiets down the room.

"We need to make a decision, quickly. This is a matter that affects all of us equally, and I think it's best to take a vote," he suggests.

The voting starts, and it's a tie. Everyone looks at you. Your vote will be the tiebreaker.

IF YOU VOTE TO BUILD MORE SOLAR PANELS, TURN TO PAGE 127.

IF YOU VOTE TO BUILD WINDMILLS, TURN TO PAGE 98.

You decide to let Nico keep looking for ice on his own while you work on taking the permafrost back to base. You spend the next hour carving out chunks of permafrost with a chainsaw-like tool, and loading up a trailer with it. By the time the jumbo rover you called in arrives from base, you've got the trailer ready to haul. Soon, you're on your way back to base, feeling like you're sitting on a pot of gold.

The team is jubilant when you get back. Permafrost is a really important resource, and the construction team makes plans to head back to your site and extract more as soon as possible. And you feel great when Commander Wen congratulates you on a successful expedition.

But as the minutes go by, you start to get worried about Nico. After he left in the rover to search for ice, he hasn't checked back in. You finally go to Commander Wen to ask if anyone has heard from him.

"What do you mean?" Commander Wen asks you. "Nico didn't return with you?"

You tell him what happened, and about how you decided to pursue different priorities.

"You never should have separated!" Commander Wen says sternly. "There is safety in numbers, especially out in the harsh Martian terrain. We need to locate Nico, and fast!"

Nico isn't answering any calls, so a search and rescue

team goes out to find him. You wait on pins and needles for news of your friend. And then, finally, they return with him. He is lucky to be alive, you find out, as they rush past you to the infirmary. His space suit's life-support system had started to fail, and his body temperature had dropped so low, he was barely alive by the time he was found. His nose and toes are covered with frostbite, and it will take him months to recover. You feel terrible for leaving him. If you had stuck together, you could have helped him. Instead, you left your friend out in the cold, literally. You don't know how you'll ever be able to make this up to him. And your team will have to face the *chilling* reality that your mission is down one valuable young astronaut for the next several months.

THE END

"Excuse me, Commander, can I speak with you?" you ask.

"Sure, what is it?" he asks.

"Well, sir, I know that the greenhouse work is important, but I don't think I'm the right person for that job," you say.

"Why not?" he asks, turning to face you.

As he looks intently at you, you feel your face turn red.

"Because . . . I think I should get a field expedition," you blurt out. "Like Nico."

"Well, that's very disappointing to hear," Commander Wen says. "I picked all the assignments carefully, including yours. It was going to be a short assignment, and you were next in line for a field expedition."

Oh.

"But since you don't want to do the goat assignment, I can send you to the construction dome, where you can make bricks for building habitats," he continues.

Wow. That's not a whole lot better than goats. But even worse, now Commander Wen doesn't see you as a team player. For the rest of the mission, you always seem to be passed over for the best assignments and given grunt work. It's still great to be on Mars, but this is not what you had hoped for. And you don't dare complain again!

THE END

With your heart pounding, you guide the telerobot over to the possible stromatolite and, with the controller, command it to chisel off a section of the rock. Next, you make the robot scoop up the pieces and dump them into the rover. You spend the rest of the afternoon collecting more samples, and then head back to base with the team. As soon as you get there, you race off to search for Julie, and find her working in the laboratory.

"Julie!" you call out. "I have something to show you . . . brace yourself."

"What is it?" Julie says, putting down the compound she was mixing.

"I might have found something huge on the expedition!" you continue.

"Really? Do you have a picture?" Julie asks.

"Even better," you say dramatically, pulling the sample out of your pocket and placing it on the lab table.

You wait for her reaction, but she doesn't seem excited.

"Check it out," you encourage her.

Julie pulls on a fresh pair of gloves and puts the sample under a microscope.

"I can't tell what this is, but there's a pretty pattern on the rock," she says.

That's it?

"Wait, look a little closer," you say.

"What do you think it is?" Julie asks.

"Um. . . a stromatolite?" you volunteer.

"Well, that would be amazing. But I can't tell from this sample. Plus, I'm really surprised Ivan and Helena let you interfere with the setting. No matter what this is, it's always best to study a discovery in its undisturbed environment first."

Oops. You tell Julie that you didn't include the others in your finding.

"Are you kidding me? That's really bad form," Julie says, and you can hear the disappointment in her voice. "I guess we'll just have to go back and check out the setting. Can you take me to the site?"

No . . . you can't. In your excitement to get the sample, you didn't mark your location.

Julie is beyond disappointed now. And you can't believe you messed up so badly. Even worse, when word gets out about your poor decision making, you aren't taken very seriously by your crewmates. You aren't invited to go on more expeditions. Eventually, you volunteer to go back to the greenhouse for the rest of the mission. At least the goats are satisfied with your work!

THE END

"Are you absolutely sure you're comfortable using dynamite?" you ask Nico.

"Definitely! I've used it before," he says. "It'll be fine. Miners use it all the time to extract resources."

Yeah, but last time I checked, you were an astronaut, not a miner. You remember reading something that said only certified blasting experts should ever try to detonate dynamite, but Nico's determined to do it.

"Do you need my help, or is it okay if I stand over there?" you ask.

"I'm good! You go ahead and stand back and relax," Nico laughs. "I'll try not to blow you up."

Ha ha.

Nico rattles off a bunch of numbers under his breath as he calculates the amount of dynamite that he needs to blast the ice. He then uses a drill to make small holes in the surface, where the dynamite sticks will go.

You nervously watch, taking an extra step back, as Nico slowly unwraps several sticks of dynamite. Next, he carefully slides the sticks into the holes that he drilled and presses them in with a plastic rod. Then Nico starts to unwind the lead wires.

"All I have to do is connect these wires to the detonator and then, when we're ready, hit the button," he says.

You brace yourself as Nico works with the wires, but you soon realize that you're watching an expert in action. You find yourself starting to relax, and even moving closer to get a better look. Nico was right—he *does* know what he's doing.

The one precaution he didn't take, though, was to turn off the rover's radio transmitters to prevent the accidental firing of the detonator. As he's activating the wires, you get a call from base checking on your status. You see horror register on Nico's face as he hears the phone ringing, and you get a terrible feeling. It only lasts an instant, though, because an instant later. . .

THE END

"Hey, Doc, can I talk to you for a minute?" you ask as Cooper wraps up his work.

"Sure, superstar, what's up?" he replies, smiling at you. "You look stressed. Hope you're not too sore from today's workout."

Cooper is always so friendly. This is going to be harder than you thought! You gulp hard, take a deep breath, and blurt out, "No, it was fine. It's just that . . . I haven't seen you monitor the ventilation system, and I was wondering if you've had a chance to do it?"

"Oh, is that it?" Coopers asks. "I started it earlier, but didn't get done. I was just going to finish up right now. Is your offer to help still on the table?"

"Sure!" you reply, breathing a sigh of relief. "Sorry for checking up on you!"

"Don't worry about it. It's always better to be on the safe side. Besides, now I can get you to do the hardest part— replacing the fans," Cooper says with a laugh.

Working together, you're done with the job within an hour. Cooper logs the completed task into his log, and you're glad that you talked to him directly instead of sneaking around behind his back. Cooper's right, safety comes first, and working as a team means that you have to be upfront with each other, even if it's awkward. You're feeling pretty good about the way things worked out, and you decide to head over to the computer station to check your e-mail before bed. You find Aneesa there, talking on the phone to her mom in India.

"I promise, *Ammi,* I'm still eating enough! The food's actually *good*! I even had chicken curry for dinner," she's saying as you float by.

You make a mental note to put curry on your menu for next week. The Mars Program has come a *long* way since the early days of space travel, when astronauts had to suck food out of tubes with straws. *Bleh!* Now your crew has dozens of gourmet choices, from shrimp cocktail to lasagna to Chinese stir-fry. Most of your meals come partially dehydrated in trays. You just add hot water and then heat them up. They usually taste pretty good, you think. You also have all sorts of ready-to-eat snacks on board, like granola bars and pudding. And best of all, you have great smoothies—chocolate, strawberry, vanilla, banana, and orange—or any combination of those flavors you want. *Yum!*

Just then you notice a faint smell in the air, and it reminds you of a food from back home that you really miss—hot barbecue straight off the grill. *Mmmm.* You can imagine the charcoal burning, and biting into a nice, juicy . . . wait a minute! You shouldn't be smelling smoke! It's not just in your head—you *really* smell something burning!

"Aneesa!" you say, catching her just as she hangs up the phone. "Do you smell that?"

Aneesa sniffs.

"Smoke!" she says, her eyes growing wide.

This could be a big, no, make that a *huge* problem. Fire and spacecraft just don't mix, and you desperately hope that you are wrong.

But where is the smell coming from? You and Aneesa tear into the habitation module, and your fears come true . . .

AND IT SEEMS TO BE WORKING.
UNTIL...
WHOOSH!
IT'S GETTING WORSE. WHAT DO WE DO?

"I think we have to vent the habitation module!"
you suggest. *Venting the module* means opening a valve
that will let the air inside the room get sucked into space. It
will put out the flames immediately. But it also means that
you and Aneesa have to get back to the service module next
door, your closest exit, since once you open the vent valve,
there will be no air left in here for you to breathe.

"But we can't!" Aneesa warns. "If we vent the hab
module, we'll cut off the rest of the crew!"

That's true. The rest of the crew is on the far side of
the ship, in the command module. If you vent the habitation
module, they will be stuck where they are until you can close
the valve and fill the compartment with air again.

You desperately press the com button, trying to reach
the rest of the crew, but it's definitely broken. You wish you
could get some instructions from Commander Wen on what
to do, especially since getting in touch with Mission Control
isn't an option—it would take eight minutes for your radio
signals to get to Earth and equally long for their response to
come back. And you just don't have that kind of time with a
fire burning!

"Let's quickly go and get the rest of the
crew out! They can come help us deal

with the fire," Aneesa suggests. You'll have to fly through the flames to get to the other side of the ship, and you don't have a lot of time. Do you try to get them over here, or go ahead and vent the module, and cut them off? The flames are almost reaching the aluminum walls of the ship, and time is running out! Every second is precious. What do you do?

IF YOU VENT THE COMPARTMENT, TURN TO PAGE 159.

IF YOU TRY TO GET YOUR CREWMATES, TURN TO PAGE 118.

You spray on some extra fertilizer. Now the tomato plants should be well nourished, and you expect to see them perk up by tomorrow.

You head back to the goats, take notes like usual, and play with the new kid. He's really cute and nuzzles up to you like a puppy. You've gotten kind of attached to the goats now, and realize that when your shift in the greenhouse ends, you're actually going to miss them.

The next morning, you're worried to see that the plants are looking even worse, not better. More of the leaves have developed spots. *Maybe they just need another day for the fertilizer to kick in.*

But the following day, you're horrified when almost the entire crop of tomato plants has leaves that are covered in brown spots. Now you've got no choice but to track down Julie. Fortunately, you find out that she's closer to base now, since her expedition is almost over.

"Hi, Julie," you say, feeling nervous when she calls you back. "I'm really sorry, but there's a big problem with the garden."

"Oh no! Did the goats get into it?" she asks.

"No, not that," you reply. "I think it's best if you come check it out."

"I'll be there soon," Julie says.

You nervously pace the garden while you wait for Julie. After a few hours, you hear her steps, and before you even look up, you hear a startled cry.

"Oh my goodness! What happened?" Julie wails.

"I saw the plants had brown spots, so I gave them more fertilizer. But it didn't help," you quickly explain.

"This is clearly a case of blight!" Julie cries. "You should've gotten rid of the infected plants! Spraying them just spread the disease faster. Now the entire crop is destroyed!"

You don't know how to respond, but you sure wish you had realized the plants were diseased. Lucky for you, you've grown attached to the goats, because when Commander Wen gets word of this, you'll be stuck on goat duty for a long time. Even worse, everyone will know that you have single-handedly set back the mission by killing off so much of the food supply.

When it's time to head home to Earth, you haven't earned back anyone's trust, haven't gone on any expeditions, and haven't managed to help expand the base like you had hoped. And that's awfully hard to swallow.

THE END

"I think we should go with windmills," you volunteer. After listening to the debate, you figure it makes sense to add a new power source to what you already have.

Over the next week, construction goes well and soon there are rows of windmills ready to spin. But then, wouldn't you know it, there's . . . no wind. Actually, there's *some* wind, but just during dust storms. And when all the dust settles, the windmills get weighed down, and they just sit. You have to brush the dust off the arms, which is a lot harder than cleaning a solar panel. And the occasional Martian breeze isn't generating enough power.

You should have stuck to the tried-and-true method that worked: solar panels. Or, even better, you should have spoken up and prevented the nuke from being shut down in the first place!

In a week, the base grinds to a halt without power. Your team is forced to evacuate and is sent into orbit around Mars until the spare part for the nuke arrives from Earth, which seriously delays the mission. The disappointment you feel is one of the most powerful emotions you have ever experienced—and you wish you could somehow use *that* power to fuel the base. There would be no shortage then!

THE END

You wait in the rover for the rescue team to come get you. There's a tense silence as you and Julie sit there with nothing much to say. A few minutes earlier, you listened in as she made the unpleasant call back to base, squirming as she tried to explain to Commander Wen what happened. You felt a little bad for her, but not a whole lot. Even though you can't blame her for your being here—you did make the decision yourself—you still wish she had never invited you! Even more, you wish one of you had remembered to check the tank before leaving.

After half an hour, the rescue team arrives and fuels up the rover. On the drive back to base, you try to memorize as much of the Martian landscape as you can. You're positive that it'll be a long time before you'll be allowed to leave the base again.

And sure enough, when you're back at the central dome, Commander Wen tells you and Julie that you are banned from *any* personal rover use.

"We don't limit rover use to keep you trapped here on base. There's good reason for the policy. Rovers are extremely valuable, since their parts are all manufactured on Earth. We need to take very good care of them to make sure they last us a long time," he explains. "Replacement parts take many months to get here."

Now that you're never allowed to take a rover out, it sure feels like you're trapped on base. And, even worse, for the rest of your time on Mars, you don't seem to be able to do anything to impress Commander Wen. All the best opportunities go to other people. When your mission is over, you realize that you didn't get to do many of the things you'd hoped to do. Your list of accomplishments is painfully empty—very much like that rover's fuel tank.

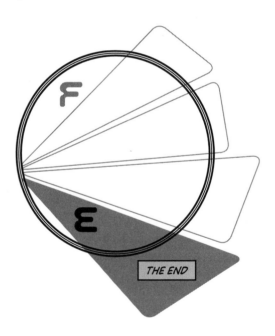

THE END

"I can't find one of the goats—she's escaped from the pen!" you confess to Julie.

"When did she get out?" she asks you.

"I'm not sure," you reply, sheepishly. "I just noticed. It could have been a while ago."

"Don't worry, we'll find her!" Julie reassures you. "Show me how she got out."

You show Julie the hole in the pen, and she helps you seal it off to make sure you don't have any more runaways. And then the two of you search the greenhouse together, section by section. There's no sign of the goat anywhere.

"What if she got out of the dome?" you ask.

"She wouldn't be able to get through one of the air locks without someone noticing," Julie says, and then her eyes suddenly go wide. "Wait a second! I hope she isn't eating my edible prehistoric plants! They have really strong scents, and you know how goats will try anything."

The two of you run over to the other side of the greenhouse, where Julie has set up a special protected section with rows of the seedlings she raised on the spacecraft. Luckily, there's no damage to the plants. At that moment, you hear a muffled bleating.

"I think the goat's behind those leaves!" Julie says. You push back the leaves, and what you see makes you gasp . . .

There's Coco, lying on a nest of leaves, with a tiny kid nestled up against her!

"Wow! Look at that!" Julie whispers.

"How beautiful," you add, slowly reaching your hand toward the pair to avoid alarming the new mother goat. She lets you pet the kid, and you marvel at the beauty of the moment. *I guess watching goats isn't all bad,* you think. Even though they can be loud and smelly, you realize that you've grown kind of attached to the seventeen—make that *eighteen* now—creatures. And who knew, even goats like a little privacy sometimes. You'll add that to your notes!

Julie helps you get the two goats back to the pen, and you both make sure that all of them are counted and fed for the night. You're really glad you asked Julie for her help, and you appreciate that she didn't make you feel bad about losing one of the goats in the first place! You're relieved that you found the goats before they got hurt, and before they caused any damage to the plants, the dome, or anything else.

"Thank you so much for all your help," you tell Julie.

"No problem! I can actually use your help with the greenhouse plants for the next few weeks," she says. "I need to go on a field mission to collect soil samples. Do you think you can tend to the vegetable garden and watch over my seedlings while I'm away?"

"Sure," you reply, eager to return the favor. Plus, since you've been reading up on growing plants on Mars while you've been goat-sitting, you can apply what you've learned.

Even though it's not the most exciting place, you know the greenhouse is a really important part of the future of human survival on Mars. Since the Red Planet is such a long way from Earth, it's way too expensive and slow to import large amounts of food, so food must be grown here. The good news is that the soil on Mars is pretty decent, and there's enough light to grow food in a greenhouse. For now, the dome you are in is pressurized to be similar to the Earth's atmosphere, and the first vegetable garden has been thriving.

The next wave of experiments will include testing to see if the lower gravity conditions on Mars compared to Earth will make it possible to grow heavier or more fruit-loaded plants, to allow for bigger crops to feed more people. Until then, the goal is to make sure that you have enough food to feed the recently expanded staff on the colony, and particularly to get a good harvest from the vegetable garden.

Taking care of the plants is pretty simple. You just need to check that the watering system is working, test the acid level of the soil, and make sure the greenhouse temperature and humidity levels are where they should be. Piece of cake! But after a few more days tending to the vegetable garden, which is mostly potatoes, beans, and tomatoes, you notice something strange about a lot of the tomato plants. Even though they've had the same growing conditions as before, you notice some brown spots on the leaves and stems. The leaves also have white dust on the edges. The plants just don't look healthy, compared to a few days ago. What should you do?

You could try to track down Julie, but she's out in the field and will be hard to reach. It might take her days to get back in touch with you. Plus, she did put you in charge of the garden, and you want to prove that you can handle the job.

You know enough about gardening to know that there are many reasons plants get brown spots. There hasn't been any change in the temperature or lighting conditions, and the watering system has been doing its job properly. You're going to have to puzzle through this. There's a gardening guide you refer to for advice, and this is what it says:

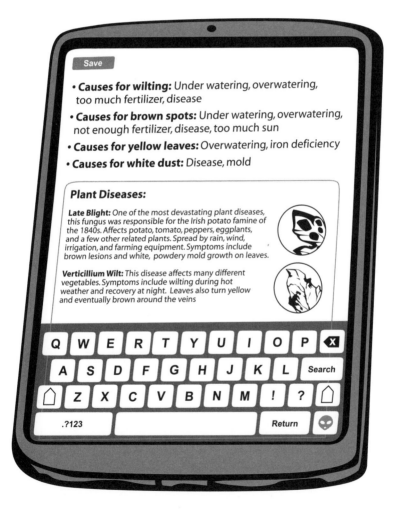

Save

- **Causes for wilting:** Under watering, overwatering, too much fertilizer, disease
- **Causes for brown spots:** Under watering, overwatering, not enough fertilizer, disease, too much sun
- **Causes for yellow leaves:** Overwatering, iron deficiency
- **Causes for white dust:** Disease, mold

Plant Diseases:

Late Blight: One of the most devastating plant diseases, this fungus was responsible for the Irish potato famine of the 1840s. Affects potato, tomato, peppers, eggplants, and a few other related plants. Spread by rain, wind, irrigation, and farming equipment. Symptoms include brown lesions and white, powdery mold growth on leaves.

Verticillium Wilt: This disease affects many different vegetables. Symptoms include wilting during hot weather and recovery at night. Leaves also turn yellow and eventually brown around the veins

After looking at the guide and thinking about the plants' symptoms, you decide there are two choices: they either need more fertilizer or they have a disease. If it's fertilizer they need, you'll spray extra nutrients onto the plants with a hose. If it's a disease, you'll have to remove all the affected plants before they infect the rest of the crop. The guide you read had a lot of serious warnings about plant diseases. It said that the diseases were very contagious, and infected plants had to be immediately removed and sealed in bags.

So, if you're right about the disease, your fast action will save the food supply from a serious threat. But if you're wrong, the loss of the tomato plants will mean less food to eat over the next few months—and a lot of raised eyebrows from your fellow Martians. What should you do?

IF YOU DECIDE TO GIVE THE PLANTS EXTRA FERTILIZER, TURN TO PAGE 96.

IF YOU REMOVE ALL THE PLANTS WITH BROWN SPOTS, TURN TO PAGE 130.

You sit down and unscrew your flashlight first. Then you disconnect the wires that power the radio to your space suit, since you're not communicating with a spacecraft anyway. It's tricky to handle the wires while working with your stiff gloves, and you fumble a bit, but you finally get ahold of them. Then, you carefully connect the wires to the terminals in the flashlight. The flashlight should be connected to the radio's power source. You flip the switch and . . . voilà! The light shines brightly! *Yes!*

Now that you've got some light, you feel a burst of energy and start to hurry back to base. You can't help but think of Dorothy and how much she wanted to get back to Kansas from Oz—and you never thought the Mars base would feel so much like home. Right now, you can't imagine being happier anywhere else in the universe. The lights get brighter as you get closer, and you can make out the domed warehouse and spaceport. You're almost there!

You burst into the central dome and find several people inside.

"Hey, everyone!" you pant, out of breath. "Our expedition team had a rover accident and Cooper and Victoria were injured. Did you guys find them yet?" you ask hopefully.

Commander Wen, Aneesa, and Julie are immediately by your side. Everyone is talking at once.

"We've been so worried about you!" Julie says. "We tried to send out a signal but couldn't reach you!"

"How did you get back here?" Commander Wen asks.

"I walked all night," you say, "using the stars to guide me."

"Wow!" Aneesa says. "That's awesome!"

You pull off your helmet and give the coordinates of where you left the stranded rover. Luckily, Nico already left a while ago with a search and rescue team, and your information is immediately sent to him.

"Copy that. We should be at their location in less than an hour," you hear Nico report back over the walkie-talkie. *Thank goodness.* More exhausted than you ever remember being, you slump into a chair, too tired to even get out of your space suit.

But pretty soon you realize that your missing expedition team isn't the only reason why everyone is awake in the middle of the night.

"We have another serious problem," Commander Wen tells you. "We received a warning alarm from our nuclear power generator. It's overheating."

"Why? What happened?" you ask.

"The dust storm," Commander Wen responds with a grimace. "The radiators are covered with a thick layer of dust, and that's causing the overheating. The wipers are too weighed down by the dust, so they can't clean off the radiators."

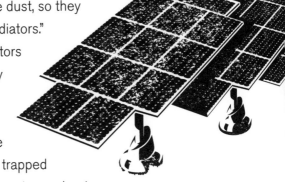

Nuclear generators have waste heat they need to get rid of to keep working. With the dust covering the radiators, the heat is trapped and causing the system to overheat.

"Can't someone just climb up there and clean off the radiators?" you ask.

"No, it's way too dangerous for anyone to go near the nuke. It's really hot, not to mention radioactive!" Julie says.

"If we can't clean them, what can we do?" you ask.

"We're going to have to activate the emergency shutdown system in a few minutes," Commander Wen says.

Wow. If the nuke is shut down, the majority of the power for the settlement will be shut off with it.

"Then what?" you wonder.

"Well, we have to get the dust off the solar panels outside, so they can start working again. And we have no choice but to operate with minimal power for a while, which will make life hard for all of us. We'll have to see if we can restart the nuke again, which will save the mission. But it's

very uncertain. It might not start back up again, or, if we don't get it right . . ." Commander Wen's voice trails off.

Yikes. You don't even want to think about things going seriously wrong with a nuclear reactor. You rack your brain trying to think of any other solution. What about using something else to clean off the radiators? Isn't there a tool or something you could use that wouldn't get affected by the heat or the radiation? Something like a . . . telerobot!

That's it! No one other than Nico knows about the new telerobot design that you were working on before you went on your expedition. The new robot has much more capability than the old ones. With your improvements, the telerobot could be commanded by remote to climb straight up the side of the radiator and shovel off the dust. Then the wipers would be able to start doing their job again!

Unless . . . what if it doesn't work? You've never tested the robot for a scenario like this—or anything close to it! And even though you've practiced with the robots a bit, and you're better at moving them around, you're not sure you're ready to take responsibility for the entire settlement, or confident enough with a robot's ability to clean off a nuclear generator's radiator. You'd feel a lot more comfortable if Nico was around to help you.

You're tempted to just let the experts handle the situation the way they think is best. They have been dealing with the crisis for several hours, and they have gone through all the scenarios at length. They might have already thought of and dismissed the robot idea, and you don't want to come across as a know-it-all. What if you use the robot and still don't fix anything, or cause damage to the radiators . . . or take too long and cause a meltdown?

It's a tough one. Your heart starts pounding as you decide whether or not to speak up.

IF YOU SUGGEST USING YOUR MODIFIED TELEROBOT, TURN TO PAGE 137.

IF YOU LET THE GENERATOR BE SHUT DOWN, TURN TO PAGE 79.

You make sure that Cooper is busy elsewhere and head over to the service module where you find Cooper's tablet on one of the consoles. No one is around, so you quickly pull up Cooper's log file.

I'm doing this for everyone's safety, you tell yourself, but you still feel sneaky going behind Cooper's back.

You check the entries for the past few days. Everything is in perfect order. According to his log, Cooper *did* check out the ventilation system earlier. And he identified the fans needing to be replaced, and scheduled the replacements for today, too.

It's pretty impressive that he managed to fit everything into his busy day—Cooper must be more on top of things than you realized or gave him credit for.

"Do you need something?" you hear as you are scrolling through the bottom of the page. You turn around, and there is Cooper, looking at you with a furrowed brow. *Yikes.* He must have wrapped up his call right after you left.

"Um, no . . ." you start to stammer.

"Why are you looking in my log?" he asks.

"It's just that . . . I was . . . I'm sorry," you continue to babble, feeling your face turning red.

"Are you *checking up* on me?" Cooper asks slowly.

"Um, yeah, kinda," you confess. "I was just wondering if

you had done the ventilation system work, since I never saw you get to it, so I looked in your file."

Gosh. That sounded really lame, you think.

"You could have just asked me directly," Cooper says. You can hear the hurt in his voice. "I would've told you the status of the job. We're all a team, and we're supposed to be open and honest with each other."

"I know. I wasn't thinking straight," you apologize. "I guess I was afraid that you'd be upset that a junior astronaut was questioning your work."

"Well, you know what? Until now, I've always looked at you as an equal on this mission," Cooper replies. "But now . . . well, now I'm not so sure."

Ouch. You hope that Cooper isn't going to tell the others about what happened, especially Commander Wen. And, more than anything, you hope that you can earn back his trust and respect . . . soon.

TURN TO PAGE 123.

"I'm going to hike back to base to get some help," you inform your teammates.

"Are you sure you're up for it?" Victoria asks.

"I'll be okay," you reply, trying to sound more confident than you feel.

"How about if I come with you?" she offers.

"That would be great, but shouldn't you play it safe and stay here since you hit your head? Plus, I'm pretty sure Cooper will need your help more than I will," you say.

"Thanks for looking out for me," Cooper replies. He's leaning on the upturned rover with his injured leg out in front of him. "I wish I could be the one making the trek. I'm so sorry, guys—for crashing and for putting us in this situation."

"There's no point blaming yourself," Victoria says kindly. "Let's just focus on getting back to headquarters."

Victoria helps you gather the things you'll need for your trek. You make sure you have the essentials, including an extra oxygen tank, water, rations, flashlight, and survival kit.

You look out into the landscape and everything looks exactly the same. It's all dusty rust-colored rocks, some pebble size, and others that are small boulders. There are no roads, no street signs, and no landmarks—but as far as you can see, you can make out the rover tracks.

"Well, I guess I'm ready to head out," you announce.

"We really appreciate what you're doing for us," Victoria says.

"Be safe, my friend," Cooper adds. Weak from the pain of his broken leg, he can't pound you on the back like usual, and instead settles for a wave. You feel terrible to see him like this, but it makes you more determined to get back to base as fast as you can. And as you start your trek, you're filled with the familiar nervous excitement you felt before your first space walk.

You head off in the direction the rover tracks take you. It's easy enough to follow the path, but not as easy to walk on the uneven and unstable rubble. After carefully making your way for about half an hour, your feet are tired in your boots,

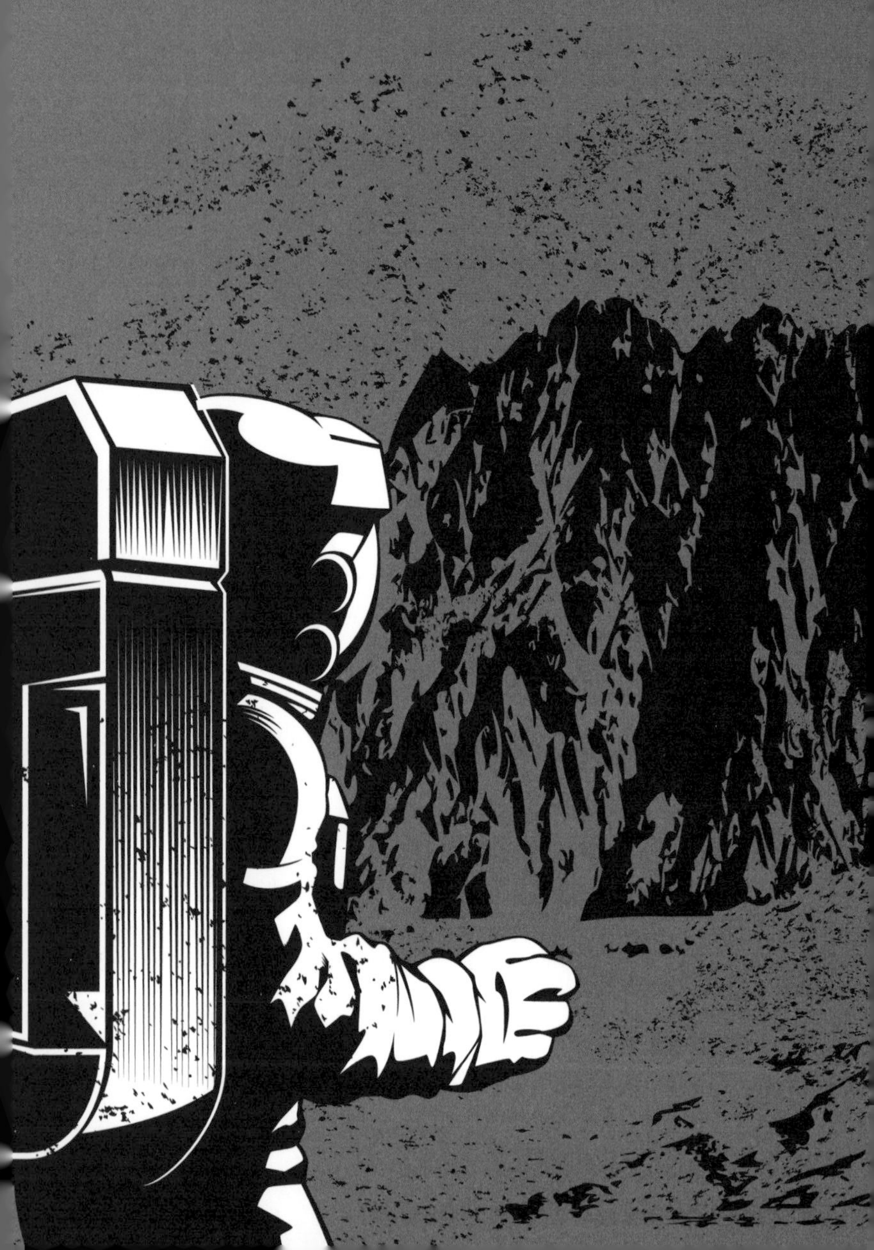

and you're grateful that you can sip water through a straw right in your helmet, and snack on a chewy energy bar that's conveniently located near your chin. Soon enough, when you have to *go*, you'll be glad your suit comes equipped with a waste collection device too!

About an hour into your trek, you notice that the air has changed, and that the wind is starting to pick up. Even though you can't feel the air through your space suit, you can see the dust on the ground stirring. You wonder if this could be the start of a Martian dust storm, which could be a really big problem! You look around and see an extra large boulder that would be perfect to take cover behind if a dust storm *does* hit. But if nothing happens, you'd just be wasting time. The other option is to buckle down and keep on walking. If a dust storm develops, you could look for cover then, or keep moving at a slow pace.

IF YOU TAKE COVER BEHIND THE BOULDER AND WAIT, TURN TO PAGE 71.

IF YOU KEEP WALKING, TURN TO PAGE 146.

YOU AND ANEESA FLY OFF TO GET THE REST OF THE CREW.

FIRE ON BOARD!

YOU NEED EVERYONE'S HELP IN THE HAB MODULE.

OH NO!

As tempting as it is to take the rover out for a spin, you decide to stick to making bricks, and go out to collect more clay for the next batch. Then, you take your time mixing the compound and pouring it into the molds while trying to stay focused. *If I never see another brick in my life, it'll be too soon.*

Gene finally finishes up with his maintenance and testing of the oven, and he gives you some tips on how to keep the oven in top working order. You can't help but wonder *should I have gone out when I had the chance?* You watch, envious, as Gene takes off in the rover. With a sigh, you head back to put a fresh batch of bricks in the oven to cook, and then take a walk around the construction dome to burn off some restless energy.

Half an hour later . . . *BRRRRRRING!* You hear fire alarms sounding! You rush back to the ovens and . . . *WHOA!* There is a blazing fire! You manage to get everyone out of the dome, through the air lock to the next dome. And you quickly call the Martian fire squad to tackle the fire.

Luckily, you reacted fast and were able to save the dome from going up in flames! Gene is sent to work in the Martian equivalent of the mail room, and you are thrilled when you are offered to take over his job . . . and his rover. *Sweet!* However, you soon realize that tooling around in the rover and performing maintenance on equipment isn't all that exciting. As the months go by, the rover loses its thrill factor since you realize you never get very far from base. You can't ever take the rover very far without special clearance, and if you bend the rules, you'll end up in the mail room with Gene! Being tied down to the job also means you aren't available for any major expeditions for the rest of your Martian stay. *Bummer!*

THE END

You get the keys to the rover, promise Gene you'll be back before he's done with his assignment, and . . . you're off! It feels amazing to be cruising around. Driving the rover is easy, although you have to be careful to steer around rocks.

You imagine yourself making a big discovery, like a source of copper. Copper ore is most likely near sites with volcanic matter, so you head in the direction of the extinct Arsia Mons, which isn't far away.

You crank up the satellite radio and are singing along when suddenly you spot . . . *uh-oh* . . . another rover heading straight toward you. You get a glimpse of the passengers, and your heart sinks. Commander Wen is waving to you, and it's not friendly. He's ordering you to pull over.

"Is there a problem, officer?" you try to joke as you stop.

"I'm sure you know that there is," Commander Wen says with a grimace. He goes on to cite your violations: You shouldn't have left your assignment, and you shouldn't have taken the rover without permission. This stunt means a suspension of all rover privileges for the rest of the mission. For the next several months, you're tied to the base, and that whole time, you pine for the Martian frontier. That's hardly worth your joyride.

THE END

Several days pass on the spacecraft, and the crew continues with the daily routine, although travel weariness seems to have kicked in. Everyone's a little quicker to get upset by something, and even the coolest personalities are being tested. Cooper isn't his regular cheerful self, which seems to have brought down everyone's mood. You're being extra careful to be as helpful and friendly to everyone as possible, and you've been focusing on your work.

Then, during the next afternoon briefing, Victoria brings up a problem.

"I just noticed that the oxygen levels on board are slightly lower than they should be. It's not a cause for alarm yet, but I wanted to let you know. I'm going to check into it and get back to you," she says.

Victoria received special training on how to use and maintain the water electrolyzer, which is your main source of oxygen on *Fire Star*. You're confident that she'll be able to fix any problems. At the same time, you can't help but wonder if the slightly decreased oxygen levels have contributed to the lack of energy you've noticed among the crew.

"I can help you work on it," you volunteer.

After the meeting, you and Victoria go to the water electrolyzer, which breaks down water into hydrogen and oxygen.

"It looks like everything is in order," Victoria says. "I'll just adjust the electrolyzer's levels a little so it produces more oxygen. We should be fine in a couple hours."

But several hours later you are in the middle of dinner when you hear *Beeeeeeeeep!* An alarm is sounding!

"What's going on?" you ask, with a mouth full of macaroni.

"Oxygen levels have dropped dangerously low!" Victoria reports. "Everyone needs to put on their reserve oxygen masks right away."

You scramble to get your mask out of your locker, and put it on. Everyone gathers in the briefing area in their masks to get more details.

"We have about twenty-four hours of reserve oxygen before we're in serious trouble," Victoria reports. "But don't worry, I'll have this resolved before then."

You head back to the electrolyzer, where Victoria starts to recheck everything again, referring to the electrolyzer manual and training materials.

"I don't understand this. The system is producing less oxygen than usual, but there's no sign of any malfunction," she tells you.

"What can we do?" you ask.

"I'm going to crank up the power and give it a few hours,

and we'll see if that helps," she replies, looking nervous.

"What if there was a small electrical short in the system somewhere? It could have caused one of the pumps to fail, which would make the electrolyzer produce less," you suggest.

"But the system is designed to show us any failures. If it was a pump or a motor, we'd see that," Victoria replies.

"Yes, but what if the electrical short is affecting the warning signals, too?" you explain.

"That's pretty unlikely," Victoria says. "Thanks for the input, but I'm just going to work on this for a while and try to figure it out."

Wow. Victoria actually doesn't seem very open to your input, but you leave the expert to work out the causes for the problem, and bump into Nico.

"How's it going?" he asks.

"Not so good," you reply. "Victoria is still trying to figure out what's wrong."

Looking at Nico gives you an idea. You read an article a while ago about making a do-it-yourself electrolyzer in a pinch. You remember the basic instructions, and if anyone on this ship can help you build one, it's Nico.

"Hey, Nico! Do you think you could help me build an emergency electrolyzer?" you ask.

"Probably. But do you think we really need one?" he asks in a worried tone.

"Let me find out," you say. You hurry back to Victoria, who's in a conversation with Aneesa about the power source for the electrolyzer.

"Hey, guys, I have an idea," you interrupt.

"What is it?" Victoria asks.

As you start to explain the do-it-yourself electrolyzer idea, you see Victoria's expression change from interest to frustration. She manages to be polite as she says, "I'm sorry, but we don't really have time for distractions right now. We'll let you know if we need your help."

Hmmm. Maybe she's right. It is a bit of a far-fetched idea, and she is the expert in charge. Maybe you should just step aside and let her handle the situation. At the same time, you can't help but wonder . . . what if they *can't* get the electrolyzer working in time? Wouldn't it make sense to at least try to build the emergency one as backup? You don't have to involve them. Should you just ask Nico to help you do it anyway, without telling the others?

IF YOU LET VICTORIA AND ANEESA HANDLE THE SITUATION, TURN TO PAGE 165.

IF YOU TRY TO MAKE A WATER ELECTROLYZER, TURN TO PAGE 167.

"I think we should stick with solar panels," you say. "We know that they work, and we can put more up really quickly."

Even though there's a bit of muttering from the people who disagree, everyone pulls together and hustles to get the new panels up. By the end of the week, you have enough power to sustain the base at a minimal operating level while the generator is evaluated further and search teams scour the landscape for geothermal power.

Even though the solar panels work, they have their limitations. It's dust storm season, so there are a lot of particles in the air. That means the panels are quickly covered by a thin layer of dust, which blocks the sun's rays. You all have to take turns going out with huge brushes to wipe off the panels, which becomes really annoying after a while.

The next week, you're walking by Aneesa and Nico when you overhear them saying "robot" and "could've prevented this problem." When you ask Nico about it, he says, "Don't you think your climbing telerobots could have helped with the nuclear reactor?"

"Yeah," you agree. "I bet they could've."

"I wish we'd thought of that at the time," Nico says.

You look away, hoping Nico won't catch the guilt in your eyes.

But he does.

"You thought of it, didn't you?" Nico asks, his eyes suddenly turning cold.

"Well, I did, but um—" you say as you search for an explanation.

"Why didn't you mention it?" Aneesa asks, looking disgusted.

All you can do is shrug your shoulders as Nico and Aneesa shake their heads in disapproval.

Soon after, you start to notice other members of your team acting a little different around you—not talking to you in the usual manner, being a little less friendly. You know that the energy crisis is wearing on everyone, and it's been stressful that it's set back your mission significantly. Plus, with the power rationing that's been put in place, people aren't able to do a lot of the fun stuff they used to be able to do to relax. You can't help but get the feeling that *everyone* knows you had a possible solution that you didn't offer. As time goes on, you definitely feel a chill in the air when you walk by the other colonists, and it's not just because the domes are heated much less than usual. The worst part is, you missed your chance to help, and you're *powerless* to change their minds about you now.

THE END

You quickly pull out all the plants that have brown spots on them, thinning the crop by about a quarter. You put aside a sample of the plants to show Julie later, carefully sealing them in a plastic bag.

"Hey, stranger, how's it going?" asks Victoria as she walks into the greenhouse. "Are you ready to get out of here? I've been assigned to do a greenhouse rotation, and you're supposed to head back to the central dome."

"Great! I'll show you around first," you offer, taking Victoria on a tour of the greenhouse. You introduce her to the goats, and then show her your log, the special prehistoric plant section, and the vegetable garden.

"Check this out," you tell her. "These tomato plants looked sick, so I pulled them out to stop any disease from spreading. Make sure you keep an eye on the rest of the crop, and make sure these bags stay sealed."

"Wow!" Victoria says. "This looks like blight—a really bad plant disease that spreads quickly. Potato plants can get it, too. Julie can confirm it, but I think you might have just saved the entire crop of tomatoes *and* potatoes!"

Your eyes go wide, and then you feel a surge of pride that makes you smile from ear to ear. Good thing you didn't wait any longer before pulling the plants, or just fertilize!

You leave Victoria and head over to the central dome,

where Commander Wen is waiting to meet with you and give you your next assignment.

"I'm hearing good things about your work," Commander Wen says. "I know you were initially hoping for an expedition, and you've impressed me with your attitude and willingness to help out. Plus, you may have saved the base from a big setback by preventing that blight from spreading! You've been in that greenhouse for long enough, and you've more than earned your place on the next expedition."

"Thank you, sir!" you reply.

"While the expedition is being organized," he continues, "you deserve a little fun."

Fun?

"What did you have in mind, sir?" you ask. Commander Wen is one of the most serious guys you know, and fun doesn't really seem to figure into his lifestyle.

"I'll show you," Commander Wen answers with a smile, leading you by the arm to a new dome that you haven't seen before.

"This is the recreation dome," he says. "It's part of the next phase of the colony. To create a healthy and happy life on Mars, colonists will need a place for sports and relaxation. It can't be all work and no play all the time."

Your jaw drops as you step inside the dome.

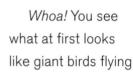

Whoa! You see what at first looks like giant birds flying around. But when you look more closely, you realize they are actually *people*, wearing huge nylon wings in bright colors strapped onto their bodies. They're flying!

"The dome's been pressurized to the Earth's atmosphere," Commander Wen explains. "Since we only have one-third of the Earth's gravity on Mars, this can allow for some neat tricks! Strap on some wings; you're taking flying lessons!"

You climb up onto a rafter and slide your arms through the giant wing straps. Next, you put on a crash helmet, just to be safe, and practice flapping your wings back and forth. Then, you step to the end of the ledge, and jump. *Wheeeeee!* This feels amazing! You've flown on airplanes before, not to mention hanging out in microgravity on a spacecraft, but there's something really special about soaring through the air like a bird! Landing is a little trickier, but you're glad the ground is padded. What a blast!

At dinner, you tell Nico and Aneesa about your

adventures in flying, and invite them to come back with you to try it out.

"Definitely!" says Aneesa. "I've been dying to go there!"

With a frown, Nico says, "That sounds awesome. I'd love to come too, but since my last expedition ended, I've been really busy with my new telerobot assignment."

Nico explains that he's in charge of repairing and cleaning the telerobots on the base. There isn't anyone else who can do the job as well as he can, and he does enjoy it. The robots are really cool, and can do pretty amazing stuff. Plus, they are an important part of the future success of the base. But it's still *work*, and you wonder if you should offer to give him a hand, so he can finish the job sooner and come try out the flying. You wouldn't mind learning more about the robots too. On the other hand, he's already had his share of adventures on an expedition while you've been stuck in the greenhouse. And now you finally have a chance to have some fun. Do you really want to give it up to do more work? You could wait to go flying again later, but Aneesa is ready to go with you now, and it would be fun to try it together.

IF YOU OFFER TO HELP NICO OUT WITH THE TELEROBOTS, TURN TO PAGE 172.

IF YOU GO FLYING WITH ANEESA, TURN TO PAGE 65.

"Okay, Cooper, we're going to go with your idea," you say. While he talks you through it, you tear off the multilayer insulation from the rover's propellant tanks. With Victoria's help, you start to wrap Cooper up like a mummy with it. Then you work on Victoria. And finally, you do the best you can to cover yourself up completely. When you're done, the three of you look like astronaut zombies. But it's working—you are nice and warm.

"Make sure to cover your hands too," Cooper warns. "Or else you'll get frostbite."

Cooper has the right idea. But what he fails to mention, unfortunately, is that you need to make sure that the exhaust line from your space suit is not covered up with the wrappings. While you and your crewmates are comfortably sleeping, the water vapor you breathe out is slowly freezing the layers of the insulation together. You don't feel it, but by the time you wake up tomorrow, your suit will just about be frozen stiff—to the point where you won't be able to move an inch. Ever wondered what it feels like to be a mummy for real? You're about to find out—the hard way.

THE END

"I think I have a way we can clean off the radiators," you blurt out, interrupting Commander Wen as he is talking to a scientist and reviewing the steps for the shutdown.

"What is it?" he asks, listening intently.

"Nico and I souped up some of the telerobots so they can do all sorts of new things. I changed one in a way that I think will make it possible to use to clean off the radiators!" you answer.

"*Hmm.* That's not a bad idea," says Commander Wen. "Quick, can you show me what the robots can do? We don't have much time!"

You both rush to the warehouse dome, where the telerobots are housed, and you show him your robot's latest moves, while he watches, impressed.

"I knew you were working on something, but this is really incredible!" he says. "I think it's worth a shot to use your robot to clean the radiators. Do you think you can operate it?"

"I think so," you reply, feeling the weight of the controller in your hand. "This is one time all my valuable experience playing video games will come in handy," you joke, trying to lighten the mood.

Commander Wen takes the telerobot outside and sets it about twenty paces from the nuclear generator. You are inside the warehouse, watching a computer monitor that shows the images from the video camera attached to the telerobot. With sweaty palms, but steady hands, you use the controller to drive the robot over to the generator. *So far, so good.* A crowd slowly gathers behind you, once they hear what's going on, but everyone is so silent, you don't even realize they are there.

YOU COMMAND THE ROBOT TO CLIMB UP THE SIDE OF THE RADIATOR.

YOU CAN FEEL THE TENSION IN THE ROOM.

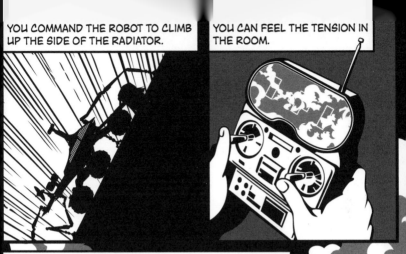

WITH A STIFF BRUSH ATTACHMENT, THE ROBOT PUSHES THE DUST OFF THE RADIATOR.

THE RADIATOR IS VIBRATING AND SMOKING!

THE ROBOT FINISHES AND DRIVES BACK DOWN.

YOU TURN AROUND AND FACE YOUR AUDIENCE.

Everyone watches, breathless, as Commander Wen tries the wipers again. They start swishing just like they are supposed to.

"*Whoo-hoo!* You did it," Aneesa says, throwing her arms around you in a big hug. Everyone in the room congratulates you and embraces each other.

"We were so nervous!" says Julie, coming up to you and giving you a high five.

"Excellent work!" adds Commander Wen. Within fifteen minutes, the reactor's warning signals are all gone. Just like that, everything is back to normal.

You're feeling pretty good about yourself, and are glad that you were confident enough to suggest using the robot. Now, once you see the rescue team get back safely, you can relax and get some sleep. You sit in a chair at Central and wait for your friends, and think about the goals of your mission.

The food supply is growing nicely, the base has been expanding, and the expeditions have resulted in good discoveries of minerals and other fuel resources. You can already imagine the future of the planet, fully colonized one day with neighborhoods and schools, telerobots running around taking care of things, and lots of recreation domes where people can learn to fly.

Although it's risky, you'd like to get back out into the Martian frontier and keep exploring. There's a lot out there waiting to be discovered, maybe even evidence of past life on Mars. But in the meantime, thanks to you and your crewmates, there will be many more people heading to Mars to build their lives here in the near future! You can't wait to share this amazing planet with your friends and family—it's been something you'll never forget!

An hour later you awake from dozing when you hear Nico's voice booming.

"There's the hero of the day!"

You look up and see Nico wearing the biggest grin you've ever seen, along with a tired but smiling Victoria. The two of them are helping Cooper stand up. You see a temporary cast on his leg.

"Hey, superstar! We hear you not only got the rescue team to us, but that you saved the base from losing power," Cooper says. "Not bad for one night's work!"

"I hope you don't mind that I used the telerobot without your permission, Nico," you say with a laugh.

"My permission? *You're* the telerobot master now!" Nico replies.

"We all owe you a huge debt," Commander Wen announces, speaking loud enough so everyone in the room can hear. "All of our astronauts are extraordinary individuals and make tremendous sacrifices for this program. But you've gone above and beyond what anyone has done on many occasions. I'm honored to be your commander and to recommend that the Junior Astronauts program be extended to other rising stars like you."

You feel your face flush as you turn red from the praise. It's an amazing feeling though—to have helped your friends, who are truly like family to you now, and to have used your skills and training to make a real contribution to the Mars Program. Plus, you've made it possible for more kids to follow in your footsteps.

"Three cheers for the superstar!" Cooper shouts, thumping you on the back. You see the smiling faces of your friends and enjoy the deafening cheers and big round of high fives.

And many months later, when it's time to head back to Earth, this moment is still fresh in your memory. You accomplished everything you set out to do, and more. Not only did your contributions get the base ready for permanent colonists, but you actually saved it from a major disaster!

As you look out the window of *Fire Star*, back at the beautiful rusty red globe that has been your home for a year and a half, you think, *I want to come back someday.*

And maybe you will!

You put your head down and keep walking. You don't want to waste daylight hours sitting around behind a rock when you could be getting closer to your goal. As you're moving along, the wind continues to pick up, and you have to use a little more energy to keep going in a straight line. Then, you look up and your mouth actually drops open. You see a massive dust cloud—one of the most terrifying things you've ever seen—heading toward you. *Oh no.*

You look for something to take cover under, or behind, but there is nothing around. The cloud is moving toward you at amazing speed, and you know you won't be able to outrun it. Your best bet is to try to let it pass over you, so you drop to the ground and curl yourself into a ball. Even through your space suit, you feel the roaring wind pounding your body with dust and pellets, and as an enormous sand dune is moving toward you, you close your eyes. Hours later, when the storm is over, the rescue team will pass right by where you are hidden from view, blended into the Martian scenery . . . forever.

THE END

After setting off in the direction you chose, you walk under the stars until you just can't go any farther. You're going to have to try to get some rest.

You manage to survive a long, cold night on the Martian frontier. Lucky for you, you had an extra battery to juice up your space suit, so you were able to crank up its internal temperature and stay warm enough not to freeze. But you were still shivering in your suit and, every couple hours, got up to dance around to get your blood pumping. The last thing you wanted was to be found as a human popsicle! It was also hard to get any sleep because of the spookiness of the Mars frontier by night. Morning couldn't have arrived soon enough.

You set off to trek toward what you think is base, still hoping for the rescue team to drive by and spot you. After walking for a while, you come to a cliff. It's really wide—about the length of ten football fields. And maybe a couple stories deep. Going around it is going to take a really long time. But going down may be slippery. You aren't thrilled about either option, but you have to choose one way to go.

IF YOU GO AROUND THE CLIFF, TURN TO PAGE 163.

IF YOU GO DOWN THE CLIFF, TURN TO PAGE 148.

You carefully slide down the side of the cliff, easing your way over rocks and making sure to step carefully. It's not that steep, so you get to the bottom pretty quickly. The crater floor is much smoother than everywhere else, so you make good time getting to the other side. Then you start the hike out of the crater. Even though it's a simple climb, you can feel your muscles burning. You are completely exhausted.

And then you see the lights of the base. At first, you think your eyes are playing tricks on you, like an oasis mirage in the desert, but as you walk on, you realize it is real. *Thank goodness!*

You stumble along, and in your haste, miss a step and *CRRRRACK!* Your ankle! A searing pain that almost makes you pass out rips through your leg.

Over the next hour, you manage to drag yourself back to base. It's painful every step of the way, but your determination to get there keeps you going.

Finally, you arrive at the central dome and crumple in a heap at the entrance. Aneesa is there, and rushes over to you.

"Oh my gosh! I can't believe you made it back!" you hear her say.

And then you black out.

. ✳ .

You wake up in a hospital bed. There's an IV line in your arm, and your leg is in a huge cast that comes up past your knee. You feel like you've been hit by a train. You look around and see an attendant.

"Where am I?" you ask.

"You're in the clinic section of the central dome."

"Did they rescue my team?" you say.

"Yes, don't worry. They were found before you got back here, and they are doing fine."

Phew. You feel a flood of relief. Your friends are okay, and you survived your trek! But the good feeling doesn't last long. You find out that your ankle has been badly broken. It looks like nothing for you but a long period of slow and painful rehabilitation over the next couple months. After that, you'll still be unable to go on expeditions, or do most of the hands-on work for the mission. Instead, you'll get to do busy work on the computer. And then it will be time to go home. The good news is that, when that time comes, at least you'll be able to walk onto the spacecraft back to Earth without your crutches!

THE END

"I'd really like to try working on my own design ideas," you say. "I think they could help make the robots even more useful."

"Sure, if that's what you want," Nico says, hiding any disappointment he might be feeling. "I'll be over here working on my project if you need my help."

You should have known that Nico is too good-natured to mind you disagreeing with him!

For the next two days, you devote yourself to working on your design changes, which include adding an extra joint to the telerobot's arms so they can move in more directions. You also figure out how to reprogram it, so the robot can use its newly improved arms to actually climb up a wall. It's pretty awesome! When he sees your robot in action, Nico is impressed.

"You might put me out of a job!" he tells you. "You're right, the robots should be able to do a lot of cool things with your design changes."

"Thanks!" you say.

Just then the phone rings. Nico picks it up.

"Hey, it sounds like your expedition team is heading out in the morning," Nico calls to you, after hanging up the phone. "You better go check in with your group. I'll finish up in here."

You are finally going out on an expedition! You rush back to the central dome, and there you find Commander Wen with Victoria and Cooper, who will be joining you.

"Glad you're here. We're ready to go over the details of your expedition," Commander Wen says as you come in.

He explains that the purpose of your field trip is to scout for alternative power sources, and that you'll be traveling in a non-pressurized rover, which means that everyone needs to wear their space suits. You can't wait. You're going to head into the great frontier of Mars for the very first time!

* ✴ ·

Morning doesn't arrive soon enough. You spent the night before preparing for the expedition, and you are now suited up, ready to head out. Cooper drives you and Victoria in the three-person ground rover, which looks like a high-tech golf cart with jumbo wheels. As you leave the settlement behind, you are impressed by the panoramic view of what has already been built. The series of domes, all connected by covered walkways, has the real feeling of a tiny city. And if your team can find geothermal power sources, which will be used to fuel more domes, it'll help the settlement expand further.

"We're going to head in the direction of the Valles Marineris," says Cooper, referring to the largest canyon in the entire solar system. "Keep your eyes open for craters!"

The surface of Mars is super-rocky, and everything is covered in a fine rust-colored powder, which is actually iron oxide. Because it never rains, the dust is always there, hanging in the air and adding to the reddish color of the sky.

"It's hard to believe that Mars is so similar to Earth in many ways," Victoria says to you and Cooper as you make your bumpy journey over the rocks, leaving rover tracks in the dust. "Mars's days are about the same length as Earth's, and it has almost the same tilt of its axis. It also has an atmosphere, different seasons, and polar caps like our planet."

"Yeah, but a year is twice as long here on Mars—and it doesn't get down to negative 90-degrees Celsius at night on Earth, lucky for us!" Cooper adds.

Even though you are in a climate-controlled space suit, you shiver to think of the incredibly cold temperatures on Mars.

For the next several hours, your team surveys the land and makes stops and takes samples where the prospect for geothermal power is likely. Then you hop back into the rover and keep going. It's tiring to be in your stiff space suit for so many hours, but it feels good to be out under the Martian sky. As he gets more comfortable in the rover, Cooper starts to push the vehicle faster and faster.

"Here we go, everyone!" he whoops.

Soon he's driving like a stuntman, flying over rocks and laughing as you cling to the handles.

"Whoa!" you yell as you land hard in your seat.

"Let's see how fast this thing can go!" Cooper says, ignoring you.

"Look out for that big crater!" warns Victoria as your rover approaches a large hollow in the ground.

CRASH!

CRUNCH!

When the rover finally comes to a stop, you're amazed to discover that you're okay. A little bruised, maybe, but nothing you can't shake off. Your crewmates, however, weren't so lucky. Cooper is lying on the ground, writhing in pain, and Victoria is nowhere to be seen.

"Victoria!" you yell.

For a terribly long moment, you don't hear any response. Then you hear a quiet moan and know, to your great relief, that Victoria is still alive.

"Cooper! Where are you hurt?" you call out next.

"My leg!" Cooper moans. "I think it's broken!"

You scramble out of the rover and try to reach Victoria on the other side. Your heart races when you see her crumpled on the ground. Could she be paralyzed?

"Can you move, Victoria?" you ask.

"Yes," she replies in a weak voice. "I'm okay, but I hit my head pretty hard. I think I blacked out. I'm lucky my helmet didn't crack!"

"We need to get you both back to base," you say.

The rover is a complete mess and isn't drivable. Your best bet is to call Central and wait for a rescue team. But, as you send distress signals through the rover, you don't get a response. The communications system, like every other part of your smashed rover, is not working.

"Where's the com cell?" you ask.

Every team that goes out on a mission is given this communications device. It looks like a big cell phone.

"It's not in there?" mumbles Cooper. "It was on the floor in the front, wasn't it?"

You start digging through the wreck of the rover. Where could it be? You search all over the crash site, and you can't find it. Could it have gotten tossed out of the rover on one of Cooper's crazy speed jumps? You start to think so.

Yikes. What now? You try to clear your head and think through your options. When your team doesn't get back in a couple hours, Central will send a rescue team out to look for

you. They should be able to find the vehicle using satellite locators. You'll just have to wait and help Cooper and Victoria the best you can until then. The problem is that it will be getting dark in a couple hours, and the temperatures will drop the later it gets. If the rescue team doesn't get to you soon, you'll have to get through the frigid Martian night.

Unless . . . what if you try to make the hike back to base on your own? You're pretty far from there, but luckily you aren't hurt. You have good survival skills and have trekked through mountains before. The tracks of the rover have left a clear path in the Martian dust that you can follow. And that way you can make sure a rescue team gets to the rover. Then again, the harsh Mars landscape is threatening, and you'd be alone.

You look at Cooper wincing in pain, and then at Victoria, who is still in a daze. You are going to have to make this decision on your own.

IF YOU WAIT FOR HELP TO ARRIVE, TURN TO PAGE 179.

IF YOU MAKE THE HIKE BACK TO BASE, TURN TO PAGE 114.

You scramble back to the service module and seal off all doors leading to the habitation module. You signal an alarm so your crewmates know there is a problem and to stay where they are. Aneesa turns a valve to vent the burning compartment, and the two of you watch in silence through a window as the fire is gone in an instant. *Phew!* Looking at the burned control panel and singed aluminum walls of the module, you realize what an incredibly close call that was. If you had waited even a few more seconds to get your crewmates, the fire would have easily melted a hole in the wall. And you don't want to think about what could have happened if the fire had spread further.

"That was really scary," Aneesa says, her voice shaky. "Good call with the venting."

"Thanks," you reply.

You look at the burned module and wonder how you're going to get the rest of your crew out from the command module, where they are stranded. They don't have access to food or drinking water where they are, and they'll start to get pretty uncomfortable soon. Plus, with the communications system down, they don't even know what's going on. The alarm you sounded before sealing the doors warned them not to come out of the command area, but that's about all they know.

Lucky for you and Aneesa, you are on the side of the spacecraft with all the survival essentials you need.

Aneesa is thinking the same thing. "We have to repressurize the hab module as quickly as we can," she says. Once the module is repressurized and filled with breathing air, you can unseal the doors, and the crew can safely come out.

"But what if the spacecraft walls were damaged?" you ask. The walls might have gotten warped or thinned from the heat of the fire. And if you try repressurizing the compartment too soon, you could blow a hole in the spacecraft.

"We'll do a survey with a remote camera and use the sensors to make sure the walls are okay first," Aneesa replies. "It should be fine."

You're glad Aneesa sounds sure of herself, but *you're* not so sure about going ahead with her plan, especially without Commander Wen's go-ahead. You wish the communications system was working so you could speak to him about the process.

But that gives you an idea.

What if you did an emergency space walk to rescue your other crewmates? You could put on a space suit, do a space walk, and deliver space suits to the stranded crew members so they can leave the command module they are stuck in and come back with you. That way Commander Wen can lead the team in restoring the burned hab module, and be the one to decide when to repressurize it.

"Aneesa, I could do a space walk and get the crew," you say. "That way we can have Commander Wen and the rest of the team help us fix the hab module."

"Are you serious?" Aneesa says. "You've never done a space walk before!"

"I know, but I practiced walks underwater during training

and through virtual reality software," you reply. "Everyone has to try it for real sometime."

"But you haven't had a chance to go through all the pre-space-walk preparations, which makes it riskier for you than usual. Are you sure you want to take the chance?" she asks.

Even as she's cautioning you, you can hear the hope in Aneesa's voice that your plan might work—and solve the problem of getting the crew back. At the same time, maybe she's right, and it is too dangerous for you to do the space walk in a hurry, without all the usual preparations. The idea of rushing into your very first space walk makes your stomach churn. Yet you're not comfortable about going ahead and repressurizing the module either. What if you guys mess up?

Right now you have to make a choice. Do you work with Aneesa to repressurize the module, or do you go on a space walk to bring back the crew?

IF YOU WORK TO REPRESSURIZE THE MODULE, TURN TO PAGE 44.

IF YOU TAKE YOUR FIRST SPACE WALK TO BRING SPACE SUITS TO YOUR TRAPPED CREWMATES, TURN TO PAGE 52.

You start your way around the cliff. The rocky terrain of Mars seemed a whole lot more scenic when you weren't stranded on it for as long as you have been. Now you're sick of looking at dust and rubble. You miss the grass and greenery of Earth, and you imagine being at the beach, splashing in the water and feeling the sun on your face.

You kick up some Martian stones with your space boot and wonder what resources might be lying around that you and your team haven't had a chance to discover yet. At the moment, you don't even care. You just want to get back to base. But the cliff seems to be getting wider with each step you take!

As you trudge along, you start to feel a little light-headed. Is this fatigue setting in? The energy bar you had is long gone, and you haven't had a meal in twelve hours. Plus, you've been walking for what seems like forever. A few moments later, you feel short of breath and a headache coming on, and you are forced to stop and sit down. *Beep!* You look down at your suit. Warning: low oxygen.

You tap at it, but there's no mistaking this signal. Your tank is low—which means you are running out of oxygen! This trek has taken way longer than you ever expected, or are outfitted for, and your tank is going to be empty in a few minutes. You take a few final deep breaths as you start to feel even more light-headed and, after a minute . . . black out.

THE END

You leave the area to let Victoria and Aneesa work on the electrolyzer. But you can't help but fidget as you wait and keep watching the clock. Victoria said you only had twenty-four hours of reserve oxygen, and then things get really critical. Twenty-two hours to go.

After nervously checking the other systems on board the spacecraft and trying to stay out of the way for the next couple hours, you head back to where Victoria and Aneesa are, to peek in and see if you can lend a hand. Victoria sees you looking in and gives you thumbs-up.

"I think we're almost there," she says. "We might have figured out the problem."

"Great! Just give me a shout if you need my help," you reply. You start to relax a little and decide to catch up on some reading, to help you take your mind off things.

You realize you must have drifted off to sleep when you suddenly awaken to the sound of another *BEEEEEEEEEEEEEEEEP!*

The reserve oxygen is running out!

You rush over to the electrolyzer and find the rest of the crew crowded around Victoria and Aneesa.

"I thought we got it working again, but something isn't right," Victoria says in a panicked voice. "I don't know what else we can do!"

"How about if I try to build that emergency electrolyzer?" you suggest.

"Yes, please!" says Commander Wen. "Why didn't you try that hours ago?"

You look over at Victoria, who mouths a big "sorry" to you. But *sorry* isn't going to cut it. Although you and Nico make a valiant effort to pull off the fastest do-it-yourself electrolyzer in history, you just don't have enough time. You take a deep breath, while you still can.

THE END

"Hey, Nico, I think we should try to make the water electrolyzer, just in case," you whisper to your friend.

"Okay, tell me what to do," he says. You knew you could count on Nico!

The water electrolyzer is going to split the oxygen out of water and store it. You explain the steps: You'll fill a container with water and mix the right amount of sodium hydroxide, an electrolyte, into it. Then you'll connect two leads to a battery and put the ends of the leads into the water. After bubbles form on each lead, indicating the hydrogen and oxygen, you'll perform electrolysis with a Hoffman voltameter. Nico already knows that the voltameter is a series of tubes. Water and electrolyte go into one tube, and then oxygen and hydrogen gas come out of another. You connect the output tube to a tank that will store the gas.

Everything goes smoothly, and a couple hours later, you've successfully created a do-it-yourself electrolyzer! The oxygen reserves on board are slowly being replenished. You and Nico watch the monitor moving in the right direction and give each other high five! Victoria and Aneesa still don't seem close to a solution for the main electrolyzer.

"Excuse me, guys?" you interrupt as they huddle around the machine.

"We're working on it!" Victoria says, without looking up.

"I was just going to tell you—" you begin, but Victoria cuts you off.

"We'll let you know when we've got it going again," she says quickly.

"Actually, we went ahead and made the backup electrolyzer!" you say.

Now you've got their attention.

"Is it working?" Aneesa asks.

"Yup," Nico says, barely containing his glee.

"Oh, thank goodness!" Victoria shouts.

"We're still hours away from fixing this thing!" Aneesa adds.

"Well, now you can relax and take your time," you say, relieved you went ahead with the plan. And so is everyone else, because the others aren't able to get the main electrolyzer fixed until after things would have gotten really dicey. The good news is, they *do* get it fixed eventually, and you can all breathe easy the rest of the journey to Mars.

CONTINUE ON TO PAGE 169.

It's been three months since your landing on Mars. You've gotten into the routine of living and working on the base, but still, at some point during each day, you stop for a second and look around, marveling that you're really here.

Surprisingly, getting settled and making the base feel like home has been pretty easy. The colonists you've met are friendly, and with so much work to do, the days are just flying by. Your first assignment has been to work with Julie, to help construct the domes that make up the heart of the colony.

There are several domes already—the spaceport where you landed, the central dome, the greenhouse dome, the warehouse dome, and more. All of them are connected, creating a little town where you can work, live, and play without having to go out into the Martian frontier.

But the downside is—you've been dying to get out into the Martian frontier! Other team members have been out on field expeditions, scouting for resources, collecting samples, and surveying the landscape. You know your construction work is no less important—and you're excited to help build the first dedicated medical dome—but you find yourself complaining to Julie that you're itching to get some Martian dust on your boots!

And then, a few days later, Julie approaches you.

"Hey, listen. I have access to a rover, and I want to get

out on the frontier and do something big," she says.

"What do you mean?" you ask.

"Well, as a biologist, my biggest dream is to find evidence of early life on Mars, and I have some good ideas about where there might be some fossil evidence."

"Wow," you say.

"I need a hand collecting the samples. Will you come with me? This isn't an authorized trip, so it's off the books," she adds.

Hmm. It sounds *really* tempting. You love the idea of going exploring. It's making you restless to be confined indoors all the time, and you don't know when you'll have another chance like this. Plus, what if you *do* make a really important discovery? You'd get to be part of it! At the same time, you're reluctant to go without getting authorization first. You've always tried to play by the book, and don't want to break any rules.

"You have to decide now," Julie says. "I have to leave right away, or I won't have enough time to get where I need to go."

IF YOU DECIDE TO GO WITH JULIE, TURN TO PAGE 182.

IF YOU PASS AND KEEP ON WORKING, TURN TO PAGE 184.

You decide to support Nico and keep searching for ice a little longer. Since you're on the northern part of the planet, the odds of finding ice here are higher. You concentrate your search in shaded areas, like crater crevices and caverns. It turns out that Nico's scouting instincts are really good— because in less than half an hour, you find a big ice deposit!

"You rock, Nico!" you say. "This is great!"

"We'll both really rock when we drive back into base with a big chunk of ice!" Nico replies with a grin.

Nico's right. The ice is no good to you as a discovery alone—the key is to get it back to base so it can be used. You thought you'd just mark the spot and have another team come back to extract it. But, as usual, Nico has bigger ideas: explosives.

"We can use the dynamite I brought to blast off a piece to show everyone," he suggests.

You're not so sure. Dynamite is a highly unstable substance, and you've never used it before. A lot of things could go wrong. But Nico's extremely confident. And he *is* a mechanical mastermind . . .

IF YOU SKIP THE DYNAMITE AND MARK THE LOCATION OF THE ICE FOR ANOTHER TEAM, TURN TO PAGE 43.

IF YOU USE THE DYNAMITE TO BREAK THE ICE, TURN TO PAGE 87.

"Hey, Nico, if you think it'll help, I can give you a hand tomorrow morning with the telerobots," you offer.

Nico's face lights up. "That's so cool of you," he responds. "Thanks!"

Early the next morning, you join Nico in the warehouse dome where the telerobots are laid out in a row. *Telerobot* is just a fancy name for robots that are controlled by humans with remote controls. They've been used on Mars since the very beginning of the planet's exploration, starting with the Sojourner telerobotic rover, which landed on Mars back in 1997 and received commands from drivers back on Earth. From then on, the use of telerobots on Mars really took off. The latest robots have better sensors, cameras, and controls, and can do much more than ever before.

"Try this one out," says Nico, handing you a controller for a robot that looks like a small tank with roller wheels, a head, and arms. "But be careful, these things are worth more than you are!"

You take the controller gingerly and slowly turn the knob, making the robot move a little. You manage to make it jerk along a crooked line, and don't let it bump into anything.

"You drive like my grandmother," Nico laughs, taking the controller from you.

You watch in amazement as he makes the robot zip

around the warehouse, making turns that would impress a professional race car driver.

"Wow!" you sputter. "I see you've played with these before."

"Sure," says Nico. "These things are amazing. But the best part is that we can always improve them and make them able to do even more."

He shows you sketches of designs he's come up with to add new features to some of the telerobots, which would make them go even faster.

"Wow," you say again. "They already go pretty fast. They'll really zoom with your designs!"

"Yeah, but I just don't have enough time to spend on the new designs with all the other work we have to do," Nico says.

"Well, I'm here to help you get through it," you reply.

After a couple days of working on the robots, you start to get the hang of them and move them around easily. You also realize that with a little creativity, you could make them do much more than just go fast. You've been thinking about some design changes of your own that you'd like to try out.

Feeling excited about your ideas, you mention them to Nico. You're surprised and disappointed when he brushes them off.

"But Nico, don't you think these changes could come in handy? Wouldn't they make the robots more human-like in their abilities?" you ask.

"I guess so," Nico says. "But let's work on these speed modifications. Then we can race!"

You're not sure what to say. Speed is fun, but you think the robots go fast enough already. And making them faster isn't really adding anything different. With your designs, you'd be able to make the robots do new stuff, and you think that's even cooler. But, you remind yourself, you're only working on the robots at all because of Nico. Part of you feels like you should do what he wants, so he doesn't get disappointed—and it *would* be fun to race. At the same time, you'd like to spend the time you have trying out your own ideas, and would like Nico to help you. You're just not sure how he'll react if you push the issue.

IF YOU AGREE TO HELP NICO WITH HIS DESIGN CHANGES, TURN TO PAGE 28.

IF YOU TELL NICO YOU'D LIKE TO WORK ON YOUR OWN IDEAS, TURN TO PAGE 150.

You're going to have to get some backup fast, before she brings down the whole dome! You should have gotten help when you had the chance. Now you've let this goat cause a lot of damage, to the mission and to your reputation. You don't know how you're going to make this up to Julie. And it looks like you're going to have to do some work rebuilding this dome. You won't be getting out of this greenhouse anytime soon. And that makes you feel pretty *baa-aad.*

THE END

You and your crewmates sit around the damaged rover waiting for help to arrive. You try to think of something to say to help take everyone's mind off the fact that you are stranded in the Martian desert, without communications capabilities, and without knowing if a rescue team is ever going to find you.

"Hey, Cooper, maybe I could beat you at one of your workout challenges now," you say.

"Oh yeah? Let's go!" he laughs weakly.

You can't think of anything else lighthearted to say. Everyone is just waiting nervously. As the minutes go by, you can't help but think about how you hope you didn't join the Junior Astronauts program only to be marooned on your first expedition and die in the Martian frontier!

It's already starting to get a lot colder. The external thermometer on your space suit reads that the temperature outside has dropped drastically over the last hour. As the minutes go by, it's going to get even colder and colder. Your space suit will keep you warm for a while, but it's going to need to be recharged to keep heating you, especially if you're sitting around. If you guys were on the move, your bodies would sweat and generate their own heat.

"If the rescue team doesn't get here soon, we're going to need to do something to keep warm," you tell the others.

"I know. I've been thinking about it. What if we plug our suits into the battery of the rover and use that for extra power?" Victoria suggests.

"But we also need to use the rover battery for light," Cooper says. "If we plug in our suits, we won't have any light, and that'll make it harder for the rescue team to find us."

Not to mention you'd be sitting in the extreme cold and darkness of the Martian night.

"Maybe we could rip the lining out of the rover's propellant tanks and wrap it around ourselves to keep warm," Cooper continues.

"I've never heard of that," Victoria says. You haven't heard of it either, but maybe it would work. The lining is made out of multilayer insulation, which could keep you warm if you wrap enough of it around yourselves.

"I won't be able to help you guys with either plan. I'm so sorry," Cooper says. He's trying not to wince from the pain in his leg, but you can see that he's really uncomfortable.

You think about everything you know about both options. You have the power of the rover to use, but it would be nice to save it for light. You could try the insulation, but you've never done it before. What's the best choice? Cooper is looking to the two of you to decide, since you'll be doing the work. You glance over at Victoria, who is rubbing her head and still looks a little out of it. She doesn't seem like she's in the best position to make the call right now. Somebody is going to have to make a decision. And right now, that somebody is *you*.

IF YOU DECIDE TO PLUG IN THE SUITS, TURN TO PAGE 38.

IF YOU USE THE LINING OF THE TANKS FOR INSULATION, TURN TO PAGE 136.

You and Julie race out to where the rover is parked. Julie takes the wheel of the vehicle, and you grip the side as she drives out into the rocky Martian terrain. It's awe inspiring! As you head away from the colony, you're impressed by how incredibly tiny you feel. All around, there is nothing but reddish dust, craters, and rocks, and pale pinkish sky.

Julie expertly navigates over to the area where she expects to find something. Since you guys aren't outfitted in your space suits and rushed out into the frontier in a pressurized rover, you'll be using telerobots to investigate for you. Julie commands a telerobot to take close-up video, while you watch on a screen. Back and forth, the telerobot moves, zooming in close any time Julie sees something promising. But, in the end, you haven't found any evidence of early life on Mars.

You try to encourage Julie on the drive back to base. "We'll keep searching, Julie, and maybe find something next time."

"It's okay," she replies. "I didn't expect to find something on the first try, but it would have been nice . . . wait! What's happening?"

You notice the rover start to sputter and slow down. The fuel gauge is almost at empty.

"How in the world are we out of fuel already?" you ask.

"I . . . um . . . didn't check it before we left. And in my hurry to get out, I forgot to take an extra tank of fuel," she replies. "I can't believe I did that."

Great! Now you're going to have to call base to get another rover out to rescue you, and get caught for leaving base without permission in the first place! Unless . . . what if you find *another* source of fuel to get you back? You passed a science station a little while ago that had a couple rovers parked outside. Maybe you could *borrow* a little fuel from them? No one would need to know! What do you do?

IF YOU TAKE FUEL FROM ANOTHER ROVER, TURN TO PAGE 78.

IF YOU CALL BASE AND ADMIT WHAT HAPPENED, TURN TO PAGE 99.

"Thanks for the invitation, Julie, but I think I'd better work on building these domes," you say. "We have a tight schedule, and I wouldn't want the mission to end with these domes still unfinished."

Even though you'd love to go exploring, you *do* enjoy your work with the engineering team. You're helping them to design the best domes for working in, living in, and playing in. The team decides what materials to use, where exactly to build, and how much to pressurize each dome. And then there's the satisfaction of seeing a new dome come to life, and knowing that you were a part of it.

But luckily, you don't have the chance to regret your decision to pass on getting off the base, because soon you are assigned to your very own expedition, to scout for water resources.

Even though no water exists in liquid form on Mars, there's a decent amount of it in the form of ice waiting to be discovered.

The more ice you can find, the bigger the colony can grow, and the less you'll have to rely on the very expensive process of making water with hydrogen from tanks brought from Earth.

You head out the next week in the rover with Nico, thrilled to be sharing in this adventure with your good friend.

Nico is confident you'll find ice—which would be a big win for your team. You hope so too.

After searching for several hours unsuccessfully, using ground-penetrating radar and other equipment, you finally strike the next best thing to ice . . . permafrost! You are ecstatic! *Permafrost* is frozen mud, which is great not only because you can extract water from it, but also because you can build with it. Permafrost bricks are even stronger than clay bricks, and after all the construction work you've been doing, you know how valuable it is. You'd be proud to show up back at base with a trailer full of the stuff.

But Nico isn't nearly as excited. "I know we'll find ice if we keep looking. I think we're getting closer," he says.

You're not so sure. It'll be getting dark soon, and you'd rather use the time to carve out chunks of permafrost than waste time looking for ice. Ice is much rarer, and you'd prefer to go back to base with something useful in hand, rather than nothing at all. Nico is insisting that if you find ice, it would be worth it!

You have a choice: you can either split up and let Nico keep looking on his own while you work to take the permafrost back to base, or you can join Nico on his quest.

IF YOU WORK TO TAKE THE PERMAFROST BACK, TURN TO PAGE 82.

IF YOU KEEP SEARCHING FOR ICE WITH NICO, TURN TO PAGE 171.

You report to the construction dome, ready to make bricks out of Martian clay that will be used to expand the colony. It's certainly not rocket science, and you're not at all excited about the work—collecting the reddish clay that is in abundance outside and molding it into bricks, and then baking them in a basic solar-powered oven. After a few weeks, you get into a rhythm and start to feel a small sense of satisfaction as you see the pile of bricks you've made growing nicely. But that sense of satisfaction doesn't amount to much, because a much stronger feeling takes over every time you catch a glimpse of the Martian frontier, and feel an overwhelming urge to get out there and go exploring. You can't help but believe that there's something great waiting to be discovered out there!

And then, the next day, along comes Gene. Gene is a staff engineer you met on the colony. He says he needs to calibrate the ovens and make some adjustments. It's going to take him a few hours, during which time you won't be able to bake any bricks. You probably should go out and collect more clay and mold bricks while you wait. Or you could offer to help out with the ovens. Or . . . Gene has a rover with him, which he drove over from the other side of the colony. What if you asked Gene if you could borrow his rover to do a little exploring on the Martian frontier? You've been working hard and deserve a break, don't you? You'll just be gone for a few hours, and no one else will even need to know. If you find something fantastic, it'll be worth it. But, leaving would mean you'd be technically going outside of your work orders without authorization. Plus, all rover outings require special permission, so they can be tracked—an annoying rule that causes a lot of grumbling on the base. Maybe it wouldn't hurt to bend the rules just this once, and you can tell Gene is pretty cool . . .

IF YOU STICK TO MAKING BRICKS AND OFFER TO HELP GENE, TURN TO PAGE 120.

IF YOU BORROW THE ROVER AND GO EXPLORING, TURN TO PAGE 122.

MARS EXPEDITION FILE

TO: ALL ASTRONAUTS
FROM: COMMANDER WEN
RE: MARS MISSION PREPARATION

This Expedition File contains maps, diagrams, images, and some potentially life-saving information you should review before our trip to Mars. Of course, we all hope we will not encounter any of the emergencies described within, but if we do, you will be glad you read this.

I look forward to our work together on this important and historic mission.

Sincerely,
Commander Wen

CC: MISSION CONTROL

**CLICK TO VIEW
DATA FILES**

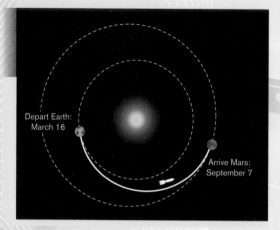

FILE 1: EARTH TO MARS TRAJECTORY

Depart Earth:
March 16

Arrive Mars:
September 7

CLICK FOR
DETAIL

NOTE
Martian day:
24 hours and
39 minutes

Martian year:
687 Earth days

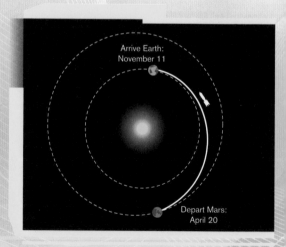

Arrive Earth:
November 11

Depart Mars:
April 20

FILE 1: EARTH TO MARS TRAJECTORY

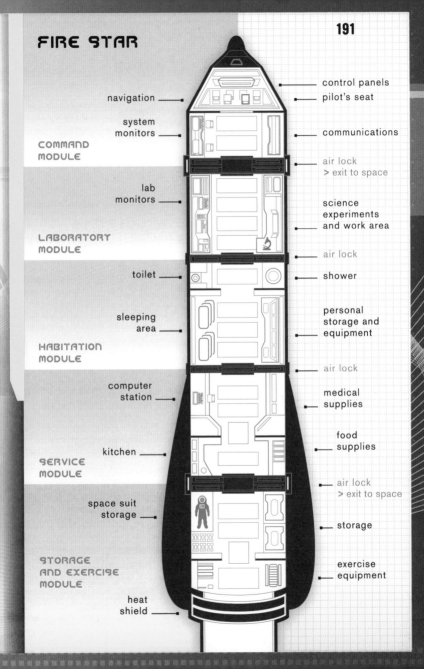

FIRE STAR

navigation

system monitors

COMMAND MODULE

control panels

pilot's seat

communications

air lock
> exit to space

lab monitors

LABORATORY MODULE

science experiments and work area

air lock

toilet

sleeping area

HABITATION MODULE

shower

personal storage and equipment

air lock

computer station

kitchen

SERVICE MODULE

medical supplies

food supplies

air lock
> exit to space

space suit storage

STORAGE AND EXERCISE MODULE

storage

exercise equipment

heat shield

MARS BASE 1
YOUR HOME ON MARS

We will spend <u>1.5 Earth years</u> on Mars, and this base will be your home. While living here, you will be working on a variety of projects to prepare the base for its first wave of permanent colonists.

Job assignments will include:
- Construction
- Administrative tasks in central dome
- Greenhouse work (crops or livestock)
- Science lab work
- Robotics (engineering or maintenance)
- Frontier exploration

We are aware that the frontier exploration assignments will be the most desirable, and we will try to ensure you each get one. However, we can't guarantee this, as we have to put our mission priorities first. As you know, for this mission, <u>construction and food source development are the two top priorities.</u>

FILE 3: TERRAIN OF MARS

BASE 1 SCHEMATICS

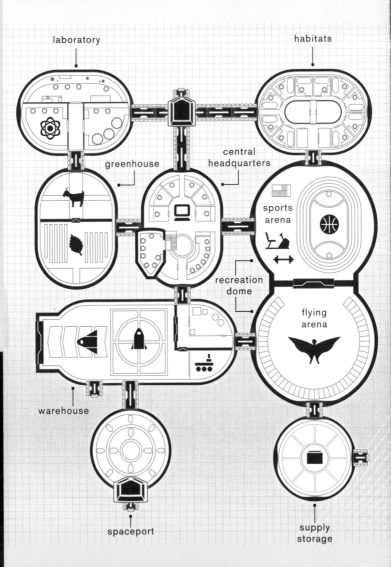

laboratory

habitats

greenhouse

central headquarters

sports arena

recreation dome

flying arena

warehouse

spaceport

supply storage

MARS:
AN EXPLORER'S GUIDE

We hope every astronaut will have a chance to take a sightseeing flight. Here's what you might see.

OLYMPUS MONS

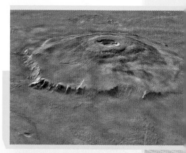

> This is the largest known volcano in our solar system. It's three times as tall as Mount Everest—but its slope is so gradual, it doesn't look very impressive when seen from the ground.

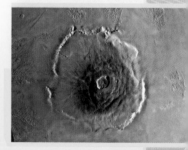

> Shaped like a thick pancake, Olympus Mons grew to its current size (about the same area as the state of Arizona) through a series of quiet eruptions with slowly flowing lava.

VALLES MARINERIS

> Valles Marineris is a set of canyons that are deep enough to hold the Alps mountain range and long enough to stretch across the whole United States!

> The canyons began as big cracks that gradually grew wider. They were shaped by wind, water, and landslides.

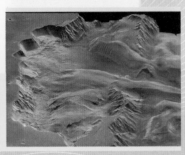

POLAR ICE CAPS

NOTE Mars looks reddish because its surface is made of iron-rich minerals that rust.

> Like Earth, Mars has two polar ice caps. Mars's ice caps are made of carbon dioxide ice, dust, and water ice.

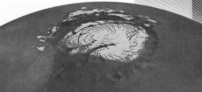

MARTIAN ROBOTS AND TRANSPORTERS

ROVERS

Telerobots: These little robots are designed to drive slowly over the rocky Martian terrain. They are equipped with cameras, drills, microscopes, scanners that detect chemicals, and arms to pick up samples.

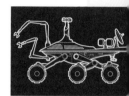

Transport rovers: These rovers are large enough to carry human passengers in space suits.

Pressurized transport rovers: The ultimate luxury in Martian land travel, these rovers have pressurized passenger compartments that allow humans to ride without space suits.

FETCHERS

These robots staff the warehouse. Every item in the warehouse is labeled with a barcode the fetcher can read. They can also respond to human commands. Just ask one to fetch you a bag of rice, and it will.

PLANES

These remote-controlled aircraft fly over the Martian terrain and take pictures. They are also equipped to carry with human passengers.

DISPLAYING LINKED HISTORICAL DATA

MARTIAN ROBOT HALL OF FAME

Our fleet of rovers and robots are the descendents of these famous ancestors.

PATHFINDER

This rover (about the size of a microwave oven) was the first to roam around the Martian frontier. It arrived on Mars in 1997 and sent 550 images back to Earth.

SPIRIT AND OPPORTUNITY

These twin rovers arrived on Mars in January 2004 and were so hardy, they lasted years longer than expected.

SCROLL IMAGES

< ·· >

How to Handle a Fire on a Spacecraft

A fire on a spacecraft sounds like very bad news, and it is. If one breaks out, you'll need to follow these steps, very fast.

Smother it

If the fire is small, smother it with one of the following:

- The thick flame-proof fire blanket provided in the emergency cabinet in each module.

- The foam-based fire extinguisher.

Both of these deprive a fire of oxygen, so it should stop burning.

Seal off and vent the module

If the fire is large, evacuate and seal off the module. Then, as soon as possible, vent the module. This will remove all oxygen, so the fire will no longer have the fuel it needs to burn.

Repressurize with care

Inspect the module for heat-damaged areas that may require repair before the module is refilled with air. Otherwise, the high air pressure may cause a hole to burst in the wall.

Survival Tips for Martians

On the Frontier

Travel in teams.
Never travel alone on the Martian frontier. If your life-support equipment malfunctions, you'll need backup.

Carry extra fuel, oxygen, and water.
To be safe, carry twice the amount you would need to get back to base.

Use rover power.
If you are stranded on the Martian frontier and your suit is running low on power, plug it into your rover.

Carry signaling markers.
These markers transmit their location to our satellites. You can use these to help search teams find you, if other equipment fails. Also use them to mark a discovery you would like to return to later.

Note: If you discover something you believe is evidence of life on Mars, it's best to mark it and leave it in place so scientists can explore its location in depth.

On Base

Know how to deploy backup power.
There are windmills and solar cells in the warehouse. Use windmills only as a last resort, as wind is rarely strong enough on Mars to generate much power.

How to Navigate at Night on Mars

The stars you'll see on Mars will look the same as the stars you see from Earth. This is because the stars are so far away from us that the distance from Earth to Mars is no big deal by comparison. The only thing that's different is the process of finding north with the stars. Mars's North Pole faces a different part of the sky than Earth's North Pole does, so if you want to find north on Mars, you'll need to follow these steps.

1 **Find the tail of the swan**

Find the constellation Cygnus the Swan, which looks like a cross. Its brightest star is its tail star, called Deneb (which means "the tail" in Arabic).

2 **Find the king's brightest star**

Near Cygnus is the constellation Cepheus, which is named for a king. The brightest star in Cepheus is Alderamin (which means "the right arm").

3 **Find the middle point**

Find the point exactly halfway between Deneb and Alderamin. That spot in the sky is directly over the Martian North Pole, which means that direction is north. That also means that south is behind you, west is to your left, and east is to your right.

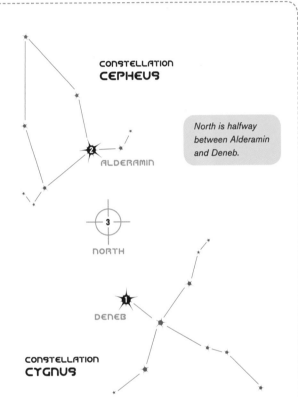

CONSTELLATION
CEPHEUS

North is halfway between Alderamin and Deneb.

ALDERAMIN

3
NORTH

DENEB

CONSTELLATION
CYGNUS

Be Aware: Mars can be an extraordinarily dark place at night, as its two small moons don't give off much light. Always carry a small light to help you avoid rocks and other hazards.

How to Survive a Martian Dust Storm

The best way to survive a Martian dust storm is to be inside the base when one happens. The only trouble is, no one knows how to predict these storms, so it's very possible to get surprised by one. Here's what to do if you're out on the frontier when the dust starts swirling . . .

Run for it

You may be able to see a dust storm approaching—it'll look like a billowing cloud on the horizon. If safe shelter is a short distance away, run for it. Or, better yet, hop into your rover and make fast tracks to base.

If you can't make it back to base . . .

You're going to have to find a good place to wait for the storm to blow over. Once the storm is upon you, visibility can drop to zero in a matter of seconds. That means it's a bad idea to keep walking or driving. So, pull over and wait, or, better yet . . .

Take shelter behind a rock

Find yourself a rock to hide behind, the bigger the better. That way, you won't get buried in sand.

Be Aware: It's a bad idea to hide at the base of a sand dune, because that pile of sand could get blown on top of you.

Now what?

The bad news is, the storm could last for weeks, or even months! If that happens, you're going to have to hope for a lull that's long enough for a pressurized rover to come out and rescue you.

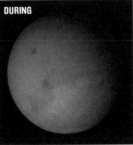

BEFORE

DURING

A severe Martian dust storm can shroud the entire planet in dust!

ABOUT THE CONTRIBUTORS

AUTHORS

Hena Khan loves the ultimate adventure of writing. She's written many books for kids, including several about space. Her favorite space experience so far was watching the Shuttle *Endeavor* launch during a visit to NASA's Kennedy Space Center in Florida. She lives in Rockville, Maryland.

David Borgenicht is the co-author of all the books in the "Worst-Case Scenario" series. He lives in Philadelphia.

CONSULTANT

Robert Zubrin is an engineer, inventor, and author who has championed research and innovation around manned missions to Mars. The founder of the Mars Society, he has developed a plan for the colonization of the Red Planet, which is detailed in his book, *The Case for Mars*. He lives in Colorado.

ILLUSTRATOR

Yancey Labat got his start with Marvel Comics and has since been illustrating children's books. He lives in New York.

The
WORST-CASE SCENARIO

ULTIMATE ADVENTURE

YOUR CHOICES. YOUR STORY. YOUR SURVIVAL.

The Worst-Case Scenario
Ultimate Adventure: Everest

YOU are about to join the youngest team ever to climb the tallest mountain on the planet. But will you set a new world record—and reach the summit alive?

THINK FAST! On Mount Everest, every second counts, and it's up to you to decide how to survive.

www.chroniclebooks.com/worstcaseadventure

DISCOVER MORE ADVENTURE
with the best-selling Worst-Case Scenario Junior Series!

NEW deluxe full-color, hardcover format!

Survival Handbook: Extreme

Survival Handbook: Junior Edition Boxed Set

Survive-o-pedia Junior Edition

Visit www.chroniclebooks.com/worstcasejunior for more information.
AVAILABLE WHEREVER BOOKS ARE SOLD.